Maureen meant what she said.
She was going to have a baby.
Somehow. Some way. Soon.

"There *are* certain criteria the man's required to meet," she told Gabriel. Her voice was calm, but her hands were beginning to flutter. "He'd have to be intelligent, gentle, affectionate. And have some sense of humor."

Gabe smiled. "Anything else? What about looks?"

She shrugged. "Well, I'm not actively looking for an ugly man, but looks aren't high on my list of priorities."

"What does top your list?"

Her eyes opened wider. "I'd think that would be obvious, Gabriel. When you ask a man to make a baby with you, the one thing he has to be is…willing."

Dear Reader,

This month, Silhouette Romance presents an exciting new FABULOUS FATHER from Val Whisenand. Clay Ellis is *A Father Betrayed*—surprised to learn he has a child and has been deceived by the woman he'd always loved.

Long Lost Husband is a dramatic new romance from favorite author Joleen Daniels. Andrea Ballanger thought her ex-husband, Travis Hunter, had been killed in the line of duty. But then she learned Travis was very much alive....

Bachelor at the Wedding continues Sandra Steffen's heartwarming WEDDING WAGER series about three brothers who vow they'll never say "I do." This month, Kyle Harris loses the bet—and his heart—when he catches the wedding garter and falls for would-be bride Clarissa Cohagan.

Rounding out the month, you'll find love and laughter as a determined single mom tries to make herself over completely—much to the dismay of the man who loves her—in Terry Essig's *Hardheaded Woman*. In *The Baby Wish*, Myrna Mackenzie tells the touching story of a woman who longs to be a mother. Too bad her handsome boss has given up on family life—or so he thought.

And visit Sterling, Montana, for a delightful tale from Kara Larkin. There's a new doctor in town, and though he isn't planning on staying, pretty Deborah Pingree hopes he'll make some *Home Ties*.

Until next month, happy reading!

Anne Canadeo
Senior Editor
Silhouette Romance

Please address questions and book requests to:
Silhouette Reader Service
U.S.: 3010 Walden Ave., P.O. Box 1325, Buffalo, NY 14269
Canadian: P.O. Box 609, Fort Erie, Ont. L2A 5X3

THE BABY
WISH

Myrna Mackenzie

ROMANCE™

Published by Silhouette Books

America's Publisher of Contemporary Romance

To Sterling—
for all the years, the love and the laughter.

And to my mother, Virginia Mackey—
who always encouraged me to chase my rainbows.

 SILHOUETTE BOOKS

ISBN 0-373-19046-8

THE BABY WISH

MYRNA MACKENZIE

has always been fascinated by the belief that within every man is a hero, inside every woman lives a heroine. She loves to write about ordinary people making extraordinary dreams come true.

A former teacher, Myrna lives in Illinois with her husband—who was her high school sweetheart—and two sons, and is the sole caretaker for a goldfish named Billy.

Lake Michigan

Des Plaines ●

Evanston ●

Oak Park ●

Chicago ●

CHICAGO, ILLINOIS
AND VICINITY

Chapter One

It was amazing how quickly a person's plans could change, Maureen "Mo" O'Shay mused, shifting in the restaurant's bright orange plastic booth. Only this morning she had been forehead deep in the final preparations for a cruise to the Greek Isles, her greatest concerns her shrinking bank account and how high an SPF her suntan oil should have. Now, scant hours later, her vacation was just a good idea that had melted away. And the way things were working out, Mo was pretty sure she wouldn't have to worry about either her pennies or getting a sunburn for the next few weeks.

She studied the plump, middle-aged woman seated across from her, and in spite of her own disappointment, Mo couldn't keep a sympathetic smile from forming. Aunt Rose looked so worried, twisting her dough-white fingers around each other as she frowned at the piñatas twirling overhead.

"Aw, Mo, I'm sorry I had to call you like this," the older woman said on a sigh. "The doctors say she'll be fine. It's just a broken leg. But with her being pregnant and all, I just have to go to her. She's my daughter, after all.''

Mo slid her hands across the varnished surface of the table and gathered her aunt's pudgy fists in her own slender grasp. ''Of course you do, Aunt Rose. A broken leg is hardly *just* anything when you're seven months along, with two children to look after and a husband who travels so much. Besides, she's not just your daughter, she's my cousin, too. Still...''

Lifting both hands in the air, Mo dropped them on the table in a gesture of resignation. The saltshaker wobbled and settled itself. ''What on earth was she doing wearing three inch heels? Pregnant women don't have to look statuesque, just serene.''

Mo raised her hands and dropped them again. Aunt Rose grabbed for the saltshaker.

''Now, Mo, you know your cousin. That's just the way she is. The point is that I've got to leave, and Mr. Bonner is out of town. I've left a message, but he hasn't called back, and...'' Aunt Rose stopped and looked straight at her niece. ''It's nice of you to take my place, Mo. I'm sure you think I should call the agency and get them to send another housekeeper, but it wouldn't be right. Not with him gone. I don't want to leave him with just anyone. Besides, there's my things. I don't like strangers staring at my things. And you, well...''

''With my schedule, I can take a cruise anytime. I can write just as well in a wealthy Chicago suburb as I can on a ship. You're perfectly right, Aunt Rose, so don't worry. I'll be fine. If there's one nice thing about being a writer, it's the fact that I'm so portable. There'll be other cruises.''

And other tans, she mused. What the heck. She always burned and peeled till she looked like a fuzzy duckling, anyway. The tan was just a whim—unimportant. Not like Aunt Rose.

The older woman stared out the window at the people who were steering past the restaurant on the sunlit pavement outside. It was an evasive gesture, one Mo recognized.

"Mo," Rose said. "About that cruise. You know how sorry I am that you've got to put off your vacation, but, well, I can't really say that I'm sorry you're not going. It's this baby thing." Rose played with her glass of water. "I hope you'll forgive me for talking to you like a mother, Mo, but ever since your friend got her tubes tied, I've been worried about you. It bothered you, didn't it, that tube thing?"

A small cardboard advertisement for thirty-ounce margaritas sat on the table. Mo dragged it toward her like a lifeline, running her fingers around the outline of the picture. "Aunt Rose, how could it not bother me? Angie's only thirty-five. I'm thirty-six. She's had four kids and now has her tubes tied, when I haven't even *used* my tubes yet. How was I supposed to feel? You know how much I've always wanted children."

And she'd been wanting them forever, it seemed to Mo. Children to love, to gift with giggles and soft whispers and silly snuggles. Children with their innocent, squishy hugs and their chocolate-milk kisses that made your cheeks wet and sticky. Mo twisted up her lips in a slight smile, remembering the dream that should already have been a reality.

"Mo... thirty-six isn't so old," her aunt said, stretching out her hand. "You've still got lots of time to find a good man and make a home."

The cardboard advertisement bent. "I don't want a man, Aunt Rose. I've had one."

"That was not a man you had. That was a jerk."

"A cute jerk." Mo knew that her flippant remark hadn't fooled her aunt, but the truth was that she couldn't talk about Richard. Not yet. At an age when she should have been wiser, she'd made a fool of herself, reading more into his caresses than had obviously ever been there, hanging on long after everything was over. And it was all too much like the way she'd chased after her father as a child when he really didn't want her around.

Well, no more. Richard had made it abundantly clear that while Mo was fun and exciting, she couldn't fulfill his social needs as a wife. And she . . . well, she'd learned her lesson once and for all. No more chasing after foolish, implausible dreams. She had a life, one she was proud of, and she fully intended to live it, happy and free of emotional complications. But that didn't mean she'd forgotten the sting of humiliation the experience with Richard had caused her.

"Cute doesn't count for much when you're a bum," Aunt Rose was saying. "And I don't want to hear that you don't want a man. You want children, but you don't want a man? This cruise . . . I was afraid that you might, you know, be planning on sleeping with a lot of men. You're like me, Mo. When you get upset, you do stupid things. Sleeping with a lot of men is very stupid."

Mo glared across the aisle at the strange woman who was staring at her and her aunt. "Aunt Rose! I was not planning on sleeping with *a lot* of men. It's true that I'm looking for a man who's agreeable to sharing his genes—a good man—but just one. And writing doesn't exactly provide a woman with a lot of golden social opportunities. The cruise was just the chance to meet someone. *One* someone," she emphasized.

"Good, because these are not safe times, Mo. I read things. I see things on TV. I was worried about you. Truly worried."

"Oh, Aunt Rose. I'm sorry if I upset you, but don't worry. I promise you, when I choose the man who could be the father of my child, I'll be very careful. The FBI's investigative methods will be nothing compared to mine. Does that make you feel better?"

"I suppose so." Rose sounded anything but convinced. She gathered her purse to her and began to open it.

Mo stopped her with one hand and pulled out her own credit card, mentally closing her mind to her dwindling savings account. This was Aunt Rose, after all. Besides, Mo thought, she was this close to making another sale. Someday soon she'd be able to make a living writing the stories she loved. She'd have enough to buy groceries for two.

"My treat, Aunt Rose," she said, reaching for the bill.

"Oh, you kids and your plastic," Rose admonished with a quick shake of her head. "Still, I guess Mr. Bonner uses those, too. He's a nice man, Mo. Have I told you how nice he is?"

Mo unwound her long, jean-clad legs from beneath her as she slid from the booth. "Many times, Aunt Rose. And you've shown me every picture the society pages have ever run of the man. Forget it, angel," she said, smiling at her aunt's pleading eyes. "The man's king of one of the most successful hardware chains in the Midwest. He's big business, absolutely socially correct. He's too much like Richard."

Besides, Mo reminded herself, she'd retired from the emotional arena. No one was going to step on her pride again.

"Oh no, Mo. No." Rose's eyes looked truly distressed and Mo cursed her own insensitivity.

"All right, you know him best, Aunt Rose. But you can still forget it. The man is notches above me on the cultural food chain. He's a totally formal type of individual, whereas I'm...a trifle unconventional. Even you've got to admit that."

"You're not unconventional, sweetheart, just casual."

Rose was looking a little nervous, and Mo understood that her aunt just wanted to make sure that things would go smoothly while she was gone, so she stifled the urge to correct Rose's last statement. *Casual* was one of the words Richard had used to describe her at the end. And he hadn't meant it as a compliment, either.

She breathed out a big puff of air as she followed Rose toward the front of the restaurant. Richard was in the past, a foolish mistake she was lucky she'd escaped from. But she'd wager that Gabriel Bonner was more of a stickler and even less tolerant of unconventional people than Richard had been. The mere fact that he was always escorting the latest "sophisticated babe" of the hotshot set said as much.

Mo sighed and wondered what idiocy had compelled her to tell Rose that she'd take on a job where she'd have to work for a man who was bound to notice her every flaw. Money, of course, was an issue. Until her cruise money was refunded or her book sold, she was nearly broke, and her next royalty check would be a long time coming. But money was always a problem when a writer was between sales. This was nothing new. She could try for another job, tell Rose she'd made a mistake....

But when she turned from paying the bill and glanced up, Rose was looking at her with those trusting, imploring eyes, and Mo remembered how many times her aunt had dried a small, lonely girl's tears when no one else had even noticed the tears were there. Growing up without a mother, and with a father who loved his sons and really didn't know—or want to know—what to do with the daughter who'd been thrust on him, Mo might have grown sullen and sad. But Rose had been there as often as she could, offering a shoulder, a smile and a quick hug when it was needed. And now, remembering the kindness that had helped her hold on to the magic of childhood, Mo patted Aunt Rose's hand.

"Don't worry about anything, Aunt Rose. I'll keep Gabriel Bonner's house going, or die trying," she promised her aunt.

It occurred to her that "die trying" was the more realistic of the two possibilities. Remembering all the pictures she'd seen of the man, all the things she'd read about him, Mo began to feel a bit like a washing machine that was permanently locked on the spin cycle. No matter what her aunt had said, after her experience with Richard, Mo knew that she and Gabriel Bonner were not going to work well together. Aunt Rose was a dream of a housekeeper—she fit the mold perfectly. Whereas Mo, well... The man was clearly not going to be pleased.

As for herself, all Mo could feel was regret over her lost week of fun in the sun. The only redeeming part of all this was that she was making Rose happy—that and the possibility that she might get a good idea for a horror novel out of the experience.

When Gabriel stepped through the door, his first thought was that if his housekeeper hadn't just lost fifty pounds and grown long, curly auburn hair, then the woman bent over the vacuum cleaner had to be the relative Rose had mentioned in her message. His second thought was that he'd obviously located the owner of the rust bucket blocking his driveway.

Gabe eyed the heart-shaped backside of the woman. There was a rip in her white denim jeans barely an inch below her bottom that allowed a touch of vulnerable creamy skin to show through. He cleared his throat, eager to get this meeting over with. After three days of emotional roller-coaster rides, all he wanted was to kick around the big house alone and let loose the feelings he'd kept bottled up all weekend.

"Excuse me," he began.

The woman straightened, kicking aside the trailing cord of the vacuum cleaner, and continued with her work.

Gabe watched as she danced the machine over the milky carpet. Her lips were moving. A slight huskiness carried over the sound of the cleaner in what some might have considered a tune. He took a breath and, in his best, booming president-of-the-company voice, tried again. "Excuse me, you're related to Rose?"

Still no response. The cleaner swung dangerously close to the leg of a table that had been in Gabe's family for two generations. Giving up any hope of communication while the vacuum was operating, he reached over and pulled the plug.

"Damn," the woman said, as the machine abruptly stopped whining. "You'd think a rich jerk like Bonner could afford a decent vacuum cleaner."

She flicked the switch back and forth a few times, shook the machine impatiently, then whirled to follow the cord. The quick movement sent her unbound breasts pressing against the jade cotton of her blouse. Gabe noted that the slight tear in the back of her pants was nothing compared to the spidery webbing of denim strands trying to hold her jeans together at the thigh.

He ought to be ashamed for staring, Gabe thought, but in his present pent-up state, he was too near the edge to keep the bridle on himself much longer.

When she saw him there, holding the plug in his hand, her face pinkened slightly. "Oops," she said, letting the cord slide from her grasp.

The plug plinked against a glass-topped table.

"You're . . . well, really, you must be—"

"It's the rich jerk in person," Gabe announced softly.

The woman closed her eyes and swallowed. "I knew this whole thing was a mistake. Of course it was. I told Aunt Rose that Oscar the Grouch was better qualified for this job than I am. But then ..." She peeked out from beneath her lashes, then opened her eyes wide. "Would it be possible—could I just start over?" she asked, wiping her hands on her jeans.

"I can't wait," Gabe confessed, leaning back against the wall, his arms crossed before him. "Why don't we start with an introduction. I'm Gabriel Bonner."

"Yes, I guessed that much," she said, looking him over. "And I'm Maureen O'Shay, Aunt Rose's fill-in. But call me Mo."

She held out her hand and Gabe took it, ignoring the soft slide of her fingers against his palm. "Mo?" he asked, letting his eyes drift over her. He couldn't imagine calling this woman something as masculine as "Mo." It didn't fit her. Even in ripped jeans she looked feminine; her limbs were long and slender. A cloud of curls encircled her slightly flushed face, falling near her liquid green eyes. She was all woman, not a "Mo," though her coloring told him that she was definitely an O'Shay.

"I'm sorry I didn't get back to Rose," Gabriel apologized, skirting the issue of her name. "But by the time I got the message I was already boarding a plane in St. Paul. Before that I was ... unreachable."

He'd been unreachable, all right, busy comforting his daughter when it was time for him to leave, trying to fit a whole month of living into three short days and then shutting the lid on his own pain as he watched her wave goodbye. When he was with Bev, his answering machine was always turned on. Still, he wished he'd known about Rose's daughter. Rose wasn't just a first-rate housekeeper. He counted her as a very good friend.

"How's your cousin feeling?" he asked. "I'd planned to call Rose later today and let her know that she needn't worry about finding a replacement to fill in while she was away. It seems I wasn't fast enough. I assume Rose gave you the key."

Gabe listened to Maureen's answers to his questions, wondering all the time what he would have done if he'd been given a choice. Would he have chosen this woman? Gabe wondered. The answer was automatic. Not a chance. He'd hired Rose because she was quiet, unobtrusive, nearly invisible, not like this beauty barely held inside her pants. Besides, Maureen "Mo" O'Shay was too young, younger than he was, he'd bet, and he had barely topped forty. He didn't need or want this kind of a distraction living in his house, especially not for the next few days, when he needed time to get his emotions back on an even keel.

"Ms. O'Shay," he began, cutting short her careful explanation about how long he could probably expect Rose to be gone.

"Mo."

"I'm not calling you Mo," he insisted. "Ms. O'Shay, it was nice of Rose to go to all the bother of finding a temporary housekeeper for me, but I really don't think this is going to work out."

"Is it because I called you a rich jerk? It is, isn't it?"

Her assumption caught him off guard, and he stood silent, one hand braced against the doorframe, the other fingering his tie.

"It is," she said with a sigh and obvious conviction. "I was afraid you wouldn't let a blunder like that pass." She bit her lower lip and studied him. "If I said I was sorry would that change things?"

Gabe studied her expression carefully. He couldn't remember ever having seen anyone who looked less sorry than this woman did. Yet, she was offering to apologize. He wondered how badly she needed this job and was hit with a smidgen of guilt. It was a familiar feeling, one he'd grown used to.

The furrow in Maureen's brow deepened as she held out her hand. "I *am* sorry, you know. I would never have made that comment if I'd...thought about it. It won't happen again."

Gabe held up a hand to stop her from going on. "This doesn't have anything to do with what you said. If you really need the work, I'm sure I can help you find another position. I'm not trying to put you out on the street."

A soft pink flush immediately began to spread over the delicate planes of her face. Maureen blinked gold-flecked lashes. Once. Twice. "I'm not sure what Aunt Rose told you," she admitted slowly, carefully, picking up a pewter figure from a table and twirling it against her palm. "But...well, I'm not *that* needy, not on the brink of taking up residence in a cardboard box yet, at any rate. Did you think I was destitute?"

The effort it took not to look down at the gaping hole in her pants was futile. Gabe tried, but the flash of skin was almost impossible to avoid. As his eyes passed her chest on the way back to her face, he again noted the softness that signaled that she wasn't wearing a bra.

"I—I do have one," she informed him as bright color splashed her cheekbones. "A number of them, in fact. I just— This isn't my usual line of work. Do you have a dress code?" she asked uncertainly. She ran one hand up and down the leg of her jeans, self-consciously.

Gabriel allowed himself one last look at those too tight jeans. "Rose usually wears a uniform," he told her.

"A uniform," she said, raising one brow. "All right. What kind of a uniform?"

"I don't know. Sort of a pink one, I think. With an apron." Gabe felt his own face growing slightly warm. Maureen was staring at him as if he'd suggested she work in a bathing suit.

"All right. You want me to wear an apron," she repeated, putting down the figurine and reaching into her jeans to fish out a pad of paper and a pen. "And a bra," he could swear he heard her whisper as she scribbled the pen in an attempt to get it to write.

"No, I don't want you to wear an apron." Why had he brought this up in the first place? It had been a rough weekend. He needed time to calm down, think rationally, get his bearings. He should have invited Patrice Munroe, his usual companion, out tonight. She was a good dose of practicality—cool, competent, beautiful enough to satisfy any man. And definitely not nearly as unsettling as this woman was.

Maureen was looking at the pad of paper questioningly. "So what do you want me to wear?" She glanced up at him.

"I don't want you to wear anything," Gabe said, allowing his voice to rise with impatience.

To her credit, though Mo's eyes rounded slightly, she didn't say a word. And she didn't write anything down. She just stood there, watching him...waiting. And then she smiled. "I'm sorry. I'm afraid I'm just not very good at this yet. So what *do* you want me to wear?" she asked again.

A long sigh escaped Gabriel. "Look, Ms. O'Shay. I'm sorry, too. And I didn't mean that last comment the way it sounded. I was merely trying to let you know that I'm not going to hire you. Sit down. Please. Let's talk. We'll straighten everything out," he emphasized.

Maureen gave a slight nod, settling herself near the edge of a sofa as she eyed its slippery white surface suspiciously. Gabriel sank down on a chair opposite her, running the fingers of one hand through his hair. This was not how he'd anticipated spending his evening.

Striving to think of her as just another employee applying for a position, Gabriel attempted to inject a business-like air into the proceedings. "First of all," he began, "just why do you want to be my housekeeper so badly in the first place?''

Startled green eyes stared back at him. Mo suddenly sat up straighter. ''Well . . . it's not exactly a question of wanting to. I don't really—'' Then, as if remembering who she was talking to, a trace of uncertainty furrowed her brow. She blinked and took a deep breath. ''What I mean is, this place is so . . . so big,'' she said with a sweep of her hand. ''And is all of it decorated in refrigerator white? Where on earth do you go if you want to eat—I don't know—Oreos? It must be a nightmare to keep clean.''

It took a valiant effort, but Gabe managed to keep from smiling. ''I'll be sure to tell my decorator you disapprove of this color scheme. She, by the way, calls this Blizzard Swirl. I'm sure it is, as you say, a nightmare to keep clean, Oreos or no. I don't eat them.''

''No, I guess not,'' she said.

He ignored her assessing tone. ''Why are you here, then, if you don't want to be my housekeeper?''

''Well,'' Maureen said, leaning nearer to him. ''I'm a writer.'' She stopped as though studying her words, then began again. ''All right, that's not exactly accurate. I'm more of a struggling writer right now. I'll admit that. But that's beside the point. I love what I do. It's hard, but it's fun, and it pays the bills . . . most of the time. The work—the money—isn't the main thing. That's not why I'm here. At least, not completely,'' she added, looking down and fingering the strands that held her jeans together.

Gabriel wanted to put his hand on hers to stop her, fearful of what might happen if any of the remaining threads broke.

''I guess,'' Maureen went on, ''you'd have to understand about my cousin and Aunt Rose and me. They're not just relatives. They're also very special people. Amy was the cousin who tried to help me hide when I got caught feeding the aspidistra my navy bean soup when I was five. And Aunt Rose was the one who declared that she'd read that navy bean soup was actually wonderful protection against aphids. A silly thing, really, but with a whole roomful of relatives witness to my crime, I was terrified at the time. And grateful that Aunt Rose understood just how much I hated that soup. Aunt Rose... Aunt Rose is like a mother to me, and she's never in my life asked me for anything till now. I just want to do something for her, give something back.... Surely you can put up with me for just a few weeks."

Gabriel wondered if she realized just how soft her voice became when she spoke of Rose, how sweetly her lips tilted. She stared up into his face, nervously waiting. Her tongue slipped out to lick her lips hesitantly. It was that simple movement that made him wonder if he could, indeed, live with this woman in his house for a period of weeks.

"Besides," she said, curling her fingers into her palms and frowning, "I gave up an important cruise to be here. Can't you just overlook whatever it is that you object to about me?"

Okay, so what was he supposed to do? His business kept him tied up. He had to have someone to help with the place, anyway. That someone might as well be this woman. All he had to do was stop staring at the hole in her pants and buy her a uniform three sizes too big and the ugliest shade of pink he could find. She'd probably fade into the woodwork easily enough then. And she'd be gone soon. He hoped.

"All right, Ms. O'Shay," he agreed. "I don't want to upset Rose, either. You've got yourself a job."

Maureen grinned up at him. "Good. Then call me Mo," she said again. "You can't continue to call me Ms. O'Shay the whole time. And only total strangers call me Maureen," she warned.

That's what he should probably call her then, Gabe reasoned. "How about Maura?"

He could have dropped an ice cube down her blouse without getting such a sudden change in expression, Gabriel figured. But she managed a tiny smile and a half nod. "If you want," she said. "It's what one of my brothers calls me. When he's angry."

It was obvious what her opinion of that name was. And that she was trying very hard to get past her aversion.

"All right—Mo," he said, giving in. "Come on, I'll take you on a tour of the house. Show you where I go when I want to eat chocolate-covered raisins."

She chuckled at that and started winding up the cord on the vacuum cleaner. "Don't bother trying to convince me you're just a regular guy, Mr. Bonner. It'd be hopeless," she assured him. "I once dated a man like you."

Now, why on earth had she divulged that bit of information? Mo wondered as she followed Gabriel into the depths of the house. To remind herself to put up a wall, was the obvious answer. And as protection against those unreadable baby blues and the play of muscles she could see beneath the white of his shirt. He didn't want her here, but she'd noticed the way he'd stared at the hole in her jeans. This man was oozing something, all right. She didn't want to give herself a chance to figure out what it was.

The thing to do now was to concentrate on not saying any more foolish things the way she had several times already. No matter what similarities Richard and Gabriel Bonner shared, they were two different men, and Gabriel was her boss. No matter what his husky voice did to her nerves every time he spoke, there was nothing personal here, nor could there ever be. She owed Gabriel Bonner and Rose her best shot. And when her aunt returned, this house would be running every bit as smoothly as it should, Mo promised herself.

She trailed Gabriel as he passed through formal dining rooms, two of them, a kitchen built to feed a small public school, more bathrooms than she cared to think about scrubbing and a pantry that didn't contain a single can of soup, her standard fare of late. Finally Gabriel paused outside a small den comfortably furnished in hunter green and polished oak.

"If you want a room to hide away in, this is the place," he offered with a grin. "Even rich jerks need to escape now and then." He stepped over the threshold and motioned her inside.

There was a feeling of home within the walls, Mo noted. Big cushy couches. Soft pillows. Lots of brass and wood, and everywhere the light scent of balsam. It was definitely a place where a person could stretch out without fear of colliding with anything. She smiled up at Gabriel, immensely pleased that here at least was a place where she wouldn't feel so awkward. But there was still something missing.

Planting her hands on her hips, Mo studied the room. "I like it. It's wonderful. But I must say it really doesn't look like anyone's been here much lately. The fireplace doesn't look as if it's been touched in years, there's no music at the piano, and the books are all sitting on the shelves. It feels . . . neglected. What I mean is, do you really live in this house," she asked gently, "or do you just come and look at it now and then?"

The corners of Gabriel's mouth turned up slightly as he crossed his arms and leaned back against the doorframe. He'd stashed his jacket and tie somewhere when she hadn't been looking, Mo noted. All trussed up, he'd been attractive—tall and striking. Now, at close range, with the open neck of his shirt revealing a slight shadow of dark chest hair and that half smile hinting at a trace of dimples, he was deadly.

"You read a room well, Mo," he offered in a voice that made her wonder what kinds of things *he* did well. "And you're right. Overseeing the operations of a business the size of Bonner Hardware takes up a lot of my life. I don't spend much of it here. You'll find you're on your own a lot."

Was that relief she felt or disappointment? Mo wondered. Perhaps it was better that she didn't know. "It doesn't matter. I'm used to being alone."

Gabriel frowned at that, and Mo thought he might be going to say something more. Instead he simply stared at her for a long moment before nodding his head toward the stairs.

"Only a few more rooms," he promised.

Mo followed along, rushing to keep up with his long strides.

The tour upstairs proceeded swiftly. The guest rooms Mo ignored, hoping she'd never have to touch them. Then Gabriel gave her a perfunctory glance at his own large suite, enough for her to see that it would be useless to try to impress a man who was essentially neater than she was.

"Felix Unger," she said beneath her breath.

"What?" Gabriel stopped beside her elbow and she realized again just how tall he was.

"You know, Felix Unger, the really tidy guy from *The Odd Couple*," she said with a whoosh of air that bounced her bangs. "That's what your room reminded me of."

Gabriel raised one brow slightly and continued on down the hall. As they neared the last room, Gabriel passed right by and began to make his way down the stairs. Apparently the tour had ended.

Mo grimaced at the thought that she had already insulted her aunt's boss before she'd even dusted a light bulb. She hung back, calling to him from the top tread. "Mr. Bonner, really, I hope I didn't offend you," she said. "Show me the last room. I'll watch my tongue," she promised.

Gabriel turned, running his hand up the rail, and shook his head. "Believe me, Mo, it would take a lot more than telling me I'm too neat to offend me. I wasn't trying to be petty. The room we just passed, well, it's just that I doubt you'll need to clean it." A muscle twitched in his cheek. "It's my daughter's, and she lives with her mother. It's seldom used. Besides," he said with a very small smile, "Bev expects everything to be just where she left it when she comes to visit."

"Your daughter," Mo said softly. She'd nearly forgotten. Yes, Aunt Rose did say something. "She's ten, isn't she?"

At the rather abrupt jerk of Gabriel's head, Mo pressed further. "Do you think... Would she mind if I just looked in once? I wouldn't touch anything. Really. I'd never move a thing."

Still Gabriel hesitated. Mo stared back at him, not sure what she expected to find in one small, absent girl's room. But there was something in Gabriel Bonner's eyes. And there was something about the word *daughter*. Finally, with a shrug, Gabe moved up the last few stairs and opened the door.

The last of the sunlight streamed in, allowing Mo a clear view of the room. Bev Bonner obviously was no dainty pink-and-white flower, it seemed. Mo's eyes widened at the bright splashes of jade and marigold that predominated the room and set the place aglow. A large plush sheepdog with a red-ribboned neck presided over a striped rug near the bed. Posters of unicorns and teddy bears shared wall space with rock stars and basketball players and a childish watercolor of a castle. Pillows were piled on the bed, on the floor and on a chair in the corner, and a waterfall of splashy ribbons cascaded down from the mirror over the dresser to brush at the golden wood below. Taped on the bottom corner of the mirror, a small photo of a family gave testament to the past.

Gabriel with his arm draped round a striking dark-haired woman, between them a young, smiling, sweet child with long dark curls and Gabriel's blue eyes. The blue-eyed imp was missing two teeth in front and she looked to be about six at the time.

"Oh," Mo said softly, forgetting herself. "She's adorable, Mr. Bonner. And I like her style, too," she said, nodding toward the many posters at the far end of the room. "You must be proud."

Mo picked up a small pillow and clutched it to her, breathing in the faint fragrance of violets. "I'm going to have a daughter like that," she promised. "Or a son. A child, at any rate. And soon, too."

A small, stifled sound from Gabriel sent Mo turning toward him. She remembered her promise not to touch and quickly replaced the pillow, smoothing it where she had squeezed too tightly.

"I'm sorry," Gabriel said. "I was assuming, Mo, that you would want room and board like Rose. It didn't occur to me that you might be married."

"I will be needing the room," she told him. "My apartment's aeons away. I've already got a friend to sublet it. As for the marriage, you were right the first time. I'm not married and not likely to be, either. At least, not in this century. It's not a husband I want. Just children."

"I see," he said, raising one brow. "Well then, if it's not too much trouble, would you mind doing me a tiny favor?"

Mo watched as Gabriel bent to smooth the fur on the sheepdog. When he looked up at her, there was a slightly harried look in his eyes. "Do you think you could try waiting until after you leave my employ before you give birth to your firstborn? I've dealt with a lot of people in my business, but I don't think I can go through another interview like this one."

Mo nodded, even though she felt her cheeks heating. Leave it to her to add an uncomfortable element to the conversation. "I'm sure I can manage to wait a little while longer."

She wondered why she had even brought the subject up in the first place and knew that it was because she had seen the love written in Gabriel Bonner's eyes when he looked at his daughter's picture. Somehow she had thought he might understand. "I'm sorry," she said. "I guess I sometimes get a little carried away when I start talking about children."

Gabriel sighed, running his fingers through his hair as he looked away and then back again, turning the full force of his gaze on Mo. "We all get a little carried away now and then," he said finally. "Come on. I'll show you where you'll sleep, Mo."

But as he rose and turned to close the door of his daughter's room, his eyes lingered on the little girl's picture. His fingers brushed the frothy butterfly hanging on the door. "Don't get too carried away, though, Mo," he said suddenly. "Children—children aren't dolls or puppies. Wanting one isn't always enough."

"I know that," Mo said a little too forcefully, studying his dark, weary eyes. "I know that a child is not a puppy."

"And you're more than a little ticked off that I dared to suggest otherwise, aren't you?" Gabriel asked with a fleeting grin as he turned to lead her down the hall. "Well, don't look so angry. When Bev was born, I didn't know. Not at all. I think I half expected her to drink out of a bowl."

Mo couldn't keep the smile from her face. "I'm sure you learned the truth quickly enough."

As Gabriel stopped outside a room and stepped aside to let Mo pass, he looked down at her. "The truth? Yes, I guess I did learn in time. The truth is that no matter how badly people want to have children, they ought to be required to

get degrees in parenthood before they produce any babies.''

Pausing just inside the blue-and-white bedroom, Mo
gazed back at him. She wasn't sure if the message was meant
as a warning to her or not. "So, did you finally get your
B.A. in Advanced Parental Studies?" she asked, avoiding
the issue of her own motherly aspirations.

But Gabriel didn't smile back as he should have. His voice
was soft and tired when he spoke. "Let's just say that I'm
still struggling to complete the course. But I have learned
one thing. No more children for me. Not ever.''

At Mo's sudden startled look, Gabriel frowned. He ran
a hand slowly over the back of his neck and blew out a deep
breath. "It seems that you've caught me at a bad time, Mo.
Forgive me. I don't usually speak to my employees this
way." Swiftly, without waiting for her acknowledgment of
his statement, he turned from her. "We'll talk more about
your duties tomorrow," he said, moving down the hall. "I
usually have breakfast at seven-thirty.''

Mo silently watched as he walked away. Turning back to
the frilly little room, she remembered Gabriel's words. He
didn't want more children. Yet his touch, his eyes, had
clearly spoken of a love for the little girl whose room was
down the hall. She didn't understand, and wasn't sure she
wanted to get close enough to ever understand.

A cruise to the islands would have been so much simpler.

Chapter Two

Mo had spent enough time alone to be perfectly at ease with her own company. She knew the value of stillness and the peaceful absence of sound. So it couldn't be the silence now that was keeping her awake, much as she'd have liked to claim quiet was the problem.

"It's him," she mumbled, sitting up in bed.

She'd already counted the patches on Aunt Rose's crazy quilt. She'd counted the stripes in the wallpaper, the leaves of the spider plant on the nightstand and the holes in the white eyelet curtains. Still, sleep eluded her.

"Gabriel Bonner," Mo whispered in an accusing tone, though she was alone in the room. It didn't matter. She'd long ago stopped worrying about the occasional sound of her own voice bouncing off the walls in the quiet. And, anyway, it wasn't the quiet that was bothering her.

It was, she finally admitted, the tortured look in Gabriel's eyes when he had walked into his daughter's empty room. It was the utter emptiness of despair that had hardened his jawline. It was the *look,* the one she recognized because she'd seen it in her own mirror at times. And it was something she definitely did not want to think about.

She didn't want to dwell on Gabriel at all. He was poison to a woman like her, and if she was very smart, and she had to be, the only thing about Gabriel Bonner that she would think about was how often he needed his socks washed.

That was it. That was all she was going to allow herself. No matter that she hadn't slept in the same house with a man in over a year. No matter that the man down the hall looked like he'd just tumbled out of the pages of *GQ.* No matter anything. For the next month or two, she was the housekeeper here, and she wasn't going to lose any more sleep over her employer or her decision to come here.

She was here now, and here she'd stay until Rose returned. Like it or not, she intended to make the best of a not so comfortable situation.

Turning to the nightstand, Mo picked up her glass of water and splashed it over the spider plant, feeling better now that she had completed another official household chore. Then she stared at it a little more closely, a frown creasing her forehead as she tried not to think of the dead begonia, the five withered dieffenbachias and the defunct you-couldn't-kill-it-if-you-stomped-on-it snake plant that had passed through her hands in the last several years.

"Try not to die before Aunt Rose gets back," she pleaded. She could have sworn she saw the plant droop a little at her words. Just as she could have sworn she heard a door open down the hall. And then another farther down. Was Gabriel looking in his little girl's room again? Wishing he hadn't lost his child?

Mo squeezed her eyes shut and ordered herself to sleep.

But sleep was slow in coming, and Mo's first conscious thought of the morning was that she hadn't slept at all.

Turning over and coming nose to nose with the clock, Mo rubbed her eyes. She looked again. The timepiece still read eight forty-five.

As she continued to stare in disbelief, the minute hand skipped ahead another notch.

"Oh no!"

Frantic, she threw on sweatpants and a torn pink sweatshirt and raced down the stairs, clutching her shoes in her hand. Hopping around, she shoved the worn gym shoes on her bare feet and sprinted out the door to open the garage.

Her ancient green Mustang sat alone.

Gabriel Bonner and his big white Lincoln were gone. He must have left without his breakfast or else he'd had to prepare his own. Either way, Mo was pretty sure that she wasn't making a very good impression on the man. Given the fact that she'd stopped knocking herself out trying to please people some time ago, it shouldn't have bothered her.

But it did.

It was 5:23 p.m. and Gabriel had been home from work only forty-five seconds, but already he'd formed what he figured was a pretty damn watertight conclusion. Maureen "Mo" O'Shay wasn't going to be like any housekeeper he'd come across this side of a television screen. That much was obvious.

He glanced around his formerly pristine living room, noting the bright baskets of silk flowers, the colorful red-and-blue throw on the couch and the clear glass bowl filled to the rim with a rainbow-hued collection of smooth pebbles.

Running his hand over his jaw, Gabe dragged his eyes away from the scene, then turned to look one more time. It wasn't that he minded a few minor changes in his decor. Hell, he could deal with that. What he wasn't sure he could deal with was the feeling that he had no control over Mo's invasion of his life. And if there was one thing Gabe knew about himself, it was that he liked to be in control.

He had only let himself drop the reins once, years ago: losing his mind when his parents and brother had died on a rain-slick highway; burying himself in the body of a woman he hardly knew in his need for human closeness; marrying in haste when he'd learned she was pregnant. He'd let his emotions run away with him. Bev had been the result, a mistake he could never regret. But she had also been the one who had to pay the price for his all too human error. And that was what made it tough to face the mirror every morning.

Gabriel placed his feet firmly on a brilliant blue Navaho rug he'd never seen in his life and glanced down the hall.

"Mo!" he called. She was back there somewhere. He could hear the steady thrum of a dance tune on the radio. Might as well go on back. It was possible, he supposed, shaking his head, that she just didn't understand that he'd like to at least be consulted before she bought new curtains for the house or started raiding his drawers and discarding his clothing.

If he hadn't been so worried about Bev yesterday, if he hadn't known that Mo was going to be very temporary, he would have already had the standard employer-employee talk with her. And it looked like he was going to have to explain a few things after all, he thought, putting his hand against a doorframe and coming away with a purple stain on his palm. Like perhaps the fact that he preferred his jelly on bread instead of his walls.

"Oh no, you don't," he heard Mo's distant voice say sternly. Gabe looked behind him, wondering if she could read his thoughts or see through walls.

Seeing no one, he started toward the kitchen. And that's when he saw it—a small cream-colored object lying just outside the closed kitchen door.

He picked it up, studying it for a second before pocketing it with a frown. What the hell was going on?

Shoving open the door, Gabe glanced around the white-on-white room, but there was no one to be seen. The song now wafting from the radio was urging him to "take it easy," but Gabe wasn't sure that he even knew what that meant anymore, or if he'd ever known. Life had not gone the way he would have wanted for the last year or so. Ever since Nora had taken Bev and moved away. And he was never sure that everything that had gone wrong hadn't been his own fault.

A small muffled gurgle came from the library as the music stopped. Ten seconds later Mo suddenly came sliding up to him, her stockinged feet slipping on the glossy bleached wood of the kitchen floor. She wore the horrid pink uniform he'd dug from Rose's closet. It was wrapped around her body twice and belted with a wide purple sash that emphasized her waist. The neckline of the gown, meant to be demure for a woman who was a size sixteen, hung indecently low on Mo, displaying more of her jiggling breasts than the manufacturer had obviously intended. Her hair was pulled up in a loose ponytail that had slipped, leaving errant burnished strands framing her face. She was a beautiful mess.

"Mr. Bonner, I'm prepared to explain," Mo began, looking up at him, her eyes widening in earnest appeal.

"Somehow I thought you would be," Gabe said dryly, letting the corners of his mouth drift up. "You might as well call me Gabriel if we're going to be so informal," he added, looking at her shoeless feet.

"I guess you're wondering what happened to your house," she continued, as though he hadn't spoken.

Gabriel touched his forehead in a sarcastic salute. "Actually, one or two questions *had* crossed my mind, but I'm absolutely positive that you're about to answer them. Now."

He draped his jacket over the back of a chair and leaned back against the wall, waiting for her to launch into her story. "So, Mo, tell me—where *did* all these things come from?" Gabe asked, motioning toward the living room.

Mo looked him full in the face, studying him. "I'm not sure you *really* want to know."

He leaned closer. "Trust me. I know what I want."

Mo shrugged, though her eyes were wide with uncertainty. "All right." She crossed her arms over her chest as if to brace herself. "I got them at my sister-in-law Cynthia's garage sale for next to nothing," she said slowly, as if waiting for the anvil to descend. Gabe could see her swallowing. "For my apartment, you understand. But since I had them, and I was here, I thought they might look nice..."

Hesitating, Mo wrapped her arms about herself. "If you want me to get rid of them, it's done. Nothing's been changed that can't be changed back in five minutes. I was just experimenting and I thought...it just seemed that...a little color in your life might not...hurt." Mo looked up at him and lifted a shoulder questioningly.

Gabriel wondered if she knew that he'd gotten more color in his life than he'd ever expected with her sudden appearance yesterday.

"I suppose it would have been better if I'd consulted you first," she added when he didn't answer right away.

Gabriel shook his head. "It's fine. Just...fine," he said, for lack of a better word.

Mo tilted her head at his comment. "Well, plain white is very tasteful," she conceded.

Gabriel raised a brow. "Mo...I think you made your feelings about unrelieved white very clear last night."

Smiling, she shrugged her shoulders. "I'm sorry. I really am. But I just can't help it. Without color a room looks so...lifeless and empty. Lonely."

She had moved closer as she spoke, and when he looked down, Gabe found that with the huge dress barely hanging on her, he was staring directly at the rounded smoothness of her breasts. A hint of her peach lace bra peeped out from the low-slung bodice of the cotton candy dress.

"You need . . . a much smaller dress," he mused, stating the obvious.

"I know," she said, taking a deep breath at his perusal, which only made the material slip more, the valley between her breasts becoming more visible. "But it seems like such a waste when I won't be here that long, anyway."

A nod was all Gabe could manage. "Well then, perhaps it *would* be a good idea to just forget the uniform after all," he agreed.

"Thank you," she said, visibly relieved. "I can't tell you how uncomfortable this thing makes me feel."

Gabe couldn't imagine telling her how uncomfortable it made him feel, either. The long column of her neck gently curved down into creamy shoulders nearly bared by the gaping neckline of the dress. This close to her, he could breathe in the fresh scent of her, and, imperceptibly, he found himself leaning closer. She looked up at him with wide, honest eyes, and Gabe forced himself to step back.

Good God, she was Rose's niece. And for the moment, anyway, his housekeeper as well. What on earth was he thinking?

He had actually almost touched her, the urge to run the tip of one finger from the shell of her ear down her throat to the shadowy space between her breasts suddenly intense, making him forget reason like a kid who's been given a cache of candy.

It had been a long time since he'd felt such a surge of desire, Gabe realized; predominantly, he was sure, because Patrice, the woman he'd been seeing lately, had asked him to be patient, and he had made it his business to be just that.

Gabe stared at the offending fingertip and jammed his hands deep into his pockets. As his fingers touched the cool smoothness of the object he'd placed there some minutes ago, Gabe recalled his earlier mission, grateful for the chance to head off his wayward thoughts.

"You wouldn't happen to know where this came from, would you?" he asked, holding the pacifier out in the palm of his hand.

Mo nearly snatched the object from him. "You found it!" she said, turning the object over in her hand as though he'd just given her a gold nugget. Quickly she moved to the sink and turned on the hot water, holding the pacifier in the gushing stream.

"That thing you're washing," Gabe said, crossing his arms as he moved up behind her. "It's a pacifier."

Mo turned quickly to look at him, her ponytail flipping back over her shoulder. Her hand remained in the water, which was starting to steam. Gabe reached around her and turned the handle on the faucet, stopping the flow. In the sudden silence, Gabe heard it again. A gurgle coming from another room.

"That's a pacifier you're holding, and pacifiers are what babies use," he prompted.

Her gaze narrowed, and Mo bit down on her lip, somewhat nervously, he thought.

"Yes . . . it is," she confessed, attempting an uncertain smile as she held the dripping piece of plastic out to him. "It belongs to Winnie." She nodded toward the other room where the gurgle was beginning to turn into more of a wail. "Otherwise known as Winifreda Alexandra Judith O'Toole."

Mo ducked under Gabe's arm and headed toward the noise. Just before she left the room, she looked back over her shoulder. "Gabriel, I'll be back in a short while to take care of whatever needs taking care of, but for now . . ." She took a deep breath. "For now I think it might be better for both our sakes if you simply stayed out of the library," she finished with a lame shrug and a pleading look.

Gabriel had no doubt whatsoever that she was one hundred per cent correct. Nevertheless, he followed Mo out of the room wondering what could top having his house turned into a garage-sale showcase.

Mo spun out of the kitchen, totally, undeniably aware of the man behind her, just as she had been totally aware of him for the last twenty-four hours. Her careful vows of the night before were meaningless. Her attempts to think of him only as an employer were laughable. For Gabriel Bonner, with his haunted eyes and his reluctant smile that brought his dimples out of hiding, was a hard man to ignore.

Damn him, anyway. The thought dropped out of nowhere. It was his fault she was feeling like a late-blooming adolescent who'd just discovered why men had slits in their briefs. But of course it really wasn't his fault. He had nothing to do with the fact that she was staying alone with a man for the first time since her relationship with Richard had fizzled. For *that* was the problem after all, she realized. It was nothing personal, nothing to be concerned about. It wasn't Gabriel's fault any more than it was his fault that he had stopped just inside the door of the library right now, his eyebrows raised to the ceiling.

She looked up at him across the cluttered expanse of the room. Gabe was tugging on his tie, loosening it as though he had a sudden need for air. Stuffing the tie into his pocket, he quickly flicked open the top two buttons on his shirt. The strong, tanned column of his throat stood out against the white of his shirt. Mo wondered that she'd ever considered plain white shirts stuffy. This one was incredibly... unnerving, especially where the open collar revealed that patch of dark curls she'd steeled herself to ignore only yesterday.

She swallowed once, hard, and then noted that Gabe was doing the same thing. Only his eyes weren't on her. They were on Winnie.

"Here she is," Mo said weakly, looking at Gabriel's wary expression and realizing only now what a supreme error in judgment she'd made.

His dark eyes gazed into her own. He swallowed again. "I see," he agreed. "And whose baby is she?"

Mo flinched at that. She remembered how she'd told him only last night how much she wanted a child, and how he'd asked her to please restrain herself while she was here.

She certainly hadn't shown much restraint or common sense when she'd said yes to her sister-in-law Cynthia's urgent request for a sitter, had she? It was true that she loved children. Mo had never made a secret of that fact. But had it gotten to the point when she would willfully think only of her own wishes? If that were true, then she was the one who was a lot like Richard, not Gabriel. He had told her he didn't want any more children of his own, and yet she had wasted no time in hustling a baby in here as soon as his back was turned. When Cynthia had asked, Mo remembered, she'd been so excited that she just hadn't thought. Or maybe she just hadn't wanted to think.

"Winnie's my niece," she explained. "I'm sorry. I was sure she'd be gone before you got here. I guess I lost track of time."

Gabe had stopped swallowing now. He nodded as his gaze traveled around his library. One dark brow lifted slightly. "I can see that things have been a little busy here," he agreed.

Mo surveyed the room. Her niece, apparently the only happy person present, leaned over the side of her playpen, peacefully attempting to devour a large soft rubber block. The second half of a gummy teething biscuit was clenched in her other fist, apparently forgotten. As Winnie paused in her chewing to gurgle a greeting to her aunt, a large glob of the teething biscuit dropped over the edge of the playpen onto Gabriel's otherwise immaculate carpeting. By morning, Mo knew, the glob would have metamorphosed into something roughly akin to concrete. If she didn't get it out of the carpeting tonight, Gabe would have to build a display case around it and call it a work of art.

"All right," Mo conceded with a groan, turning to Gabriel. "You're right. The place is a mess. There are diapers on the floor... toys, a few million cracker crumbs..." She stopped talking, watching Gabriel as he stared mutely at the disastrous shape his library was in.

Hell, she was supposed to be the man's housekeeper, not a one-woman demolition team. Nervously, Mo picked a blanket up off the floor. "Don't worry. I'll fix everything," she promised. "It won't take more than a few minutes. Right, Winnie?" she asked the baby.

Winnie smiled obligingly and threw the rest of her sodden teething biscuit at Gabriel.

Gabriel stared down at the offending mass that had hit him square in the groin and was trying to ooze its way down his leg. The fact that a part of him wanted to throw his head back and laugh surprised him. He didn't laugh much anymore. If he hadn't been so convinced that Mo would take it as a sign that he didn't mind having a baby in his house, he might have let loose the way he wanted to. But the truth was that he did mind, and as it was, he clamped his lips shut and simply stared at her.

Mo looked absolutely horrified, her mouth hanging open, her eyes bigger and rounder and greener than ever, if that were possible.

She wasn't any more comfortable with this situation they'd found themselves in than he was, he could tell that much. They were both connected through Rose, thrown together in roles they weren't used to playing. It was too obvious that she'd never been anyone's housekeeper before. And he, well, he'd had many housekeepers, but never one like this, never one like Mo, with hair that tumbled around her face in flame-colored strands, and who, it seemed, was bent on trashing his house rather than cleaning it.

Correction, Gabe thought, as Mo moved quickly across the room. Right now she was bent on...on holding a wet cloth to his pants and attempting to wipe the goo away.

"Gabriel, I'm so—so sorry," she said, biting her lip and dabbing at his crotch with the cloth. Her fingers found the spot and stroked down in long, quick movements, then up again, rubbing at the stain which was obviously a persistent one. "I'm so sorry," she repeated in a whisper that shimmied up his spine. The back of her neck glowed bright pink with embarrassment as she tried to salvage the unsalvage-able.

Gabe sucked in his breath as her hands came up against him. Once, then twice. The gasp that threatened to immobilize his lungs was quickly swallowed. His brain began to short-circuit and he ordered it to behave. She had pulled the cloth down the length of his leg and was moving back up again when he managed to grasp her wrists. For long seconds he just stared down at himself, praying for control as he struggled to find his voice.

Pulling her hands up and away, he drew her from a kneeling position until her eyes finally met his. His heart was still racing erratically when he finally found his voice, but he ignored the pounding in his chest. "Don't worry about it," he choked out.

"No," she said, shaking her head, freeing a spray of curls from her ponytail. "Aunt Rose put her faith in me. Yet I come in here, make you miss your breakfast, wreck your house, destroy a suit that probably costs more than the national debt and bring in a baby without your permission.

How can I not worry about it? I've only been here twenty-four hours and already I'm doubting whether I'll ever last out the time till Aunt Rose returns—or if you'll have any house left if I do."

Considering the fact that Gabe had been thinking the very same thing ever since he'd met her, it was hard to understand why he now felt like defending her. Maybe it was because she looked so utterly forlorn. Maybe it was just her reference to Rose. Hell, he didn't know, but she suddenly looked alone and lost and unsure of herself.

"You'll be fine," he assured both her and himself. "I'm not an ogre, Mo, or a demanding man. Rose *is* incredibly neat, but you don't have to be Rose. It's not the state of the house or my breakfast that concerns me. I can pour a cup of coffee or use the toaster when I have to, and a few billion crumbs," he said, "aren't going to make me go berserk. However, I have to insist that you consult me about a few things," he urged.

She stared at him, sucking in her lower lip, then glanced over her shoulder. Winnie had resumed chewing on the rubber block.

"Are you mad at Winnie?" she asked.

Gabe stared at the innocent, curly haired moppet who was cooing her delight as she gnawed away.

He looked into Mo's worried eyes and slowly shook his head.

Her relief was instantaneous, her smile brilliant.

"Then you don't mind so much that she's here?"

"I didn't say that," he said gently. "I didn't hire you as a baby-sitter, Mo."

"You didn't hire me at all."

"No, I didn't," Gabe said, running frustrated fingers through his hair as he readied himself for battle. "But you're still working for me."

"And you probably wish I hadn't come here at all now, don't you?" She was biting her lip again, her teeth softly indenting the fullness, then releasing the wet pink flesh.

Gabe closed his eyes. "How do you feel about being here?" he rasped. "You told me before that you didn't really want this job."

Mo clasped her arms about her and rocked side to side. "I promised I'd do this for Aunt Rose. She's counting on me, and I don't want to disappoint her," Mo reminded him.

He nodded. "Well, that makes two of us. I don't want to disappoint Rose, either. And I think you and I ought to be able to find some common ground for the short duration of your stay. But no babies. Agreed?" He smiled slightly and held out his hand, waiting to see if she could live with his decision.

She slipped her slender fingers against the warmth of his palm.

"I think I can manage not to make your life too miserable for a few weeks," she promised with a sudden smile.

Gabe released her hand then, still feeling its imprint as he pushed his own fist back into his pocket and turned to go upstairs.

"The reason you don't want any babies here," she said to his back. "Is it because you just don't like them in general . . . or is it because of your daughter?"

Her words froze him where he stood. He turned to her slowly, as though his muscles had turned to ice.

Mo's fingers were over her mouth. "Forget I asked that," she begged. "I'm sorry. It's a bad habit of mine, saying whatever I think. It works fine when I'm alone and writing," she babbled on. "Only, in public, sometimes I forget that there's no chance to go back and edit. I shouldn't have said what I did."

The woman certainly knew how to peel away the camouflage, Gabe thought. It wasn't that he didn't like babies.

How could anyone dislike the chubby-cheeked innocent who had so happily turned her attention from the rubber block to her toes and was gleefully stuffing them into her mouth? It wasn't that he didn't like her. But Gabe knew that if he watched long enough, the ache would begin to seep in and surround him. Even now, he found himself thinking that Winnie reminded him of someone who had once lived in this very house. A precious child, his Bev, grown older now. But still he remembered. He remembered. Because most of the time memories and pictures were all that he had of her. And he couldn't bear the bittersweet memories when they hit.

Looking at Winnie, listening to her contented baby noises, the universal sounds of a child who's never known true disappointment, the pain in his chest spread out like a cloud. Bev was like that. Once. Not anymore. She knew all too well the pain of disappointment these days. And knowing that he was somehow a part of that pain could nearly bring him to his knees.

Feeling the crushing weight of the guilt that never left him completely, he picked up the discarded block and turned it in his hands, staring at the thing mutely.

"I'll have Winnie home in a few minutes," she promised softly. "And dinner at six. Is that all right?"

"It's fine, Mo," he agreed, turning to her and recognizing the look in her eyes. She was concerned for him, he thought with surprise. And somehow it seemed important that he reassure her that her words hadn't destroyed the tenuous truce they'd made. "Don't worry. Everything's going to be fine."

He'd repeated the words so many times lately that they came automatically now, causing the frown between Mo's eyes to smooth a bit. Still, Gabe noted, she hadn't agreed with him, her only concession a slight nod.

This time he made it to the end of the hallway when he turned to see Mo gathering up the clutter on the floor. She paused every few seconds to say a word to Winnie, to drop a soft kiss on her curls. It was easy to see that Mo was a natural with kids. It was easy to see the love and longing in her eyes. And it occurred to him that Mo meant what she said. She was going to have a baby, somehow, some way, soon.

And yet she seemed so incredibly alone with her talk of solo vacations and her plans to become a single parent. Gabe had heard that a writer's life was a lonely one. He wondered how in touch with reality Mo really was.

Blowing out his breath in a long sigh and then sucking it in again, Gabe retraced his steps back down the hall.

"Mo?" His hand against the doorframe, his voice emerged gruffer than he had intended.

She looked up, questioning, pulling Winnie onto her hip as she waited for him to continue.

He stared at her long and hard, unsure of how to start. "Mo, when you choose the man you want to father your child, choose carefully, all right? Don't do anything rash."

Winnie was fidgeting in Mo's arms. Sliding the little girl to the floor of the playpen, Mo never took her eyes off Gabriel.

"I will," she promised. "I don't plan to rush into anything, and I *have* given this a great deal of thought. Really. There *are* certain criteria the man's required to meet."

Her voice was calm, but her hands were beginning to flutter a bit. She slid them behind her back.

"And what are your requirements in a man, Maureen O'Shay?" Gabe asked solemnly.

Her lips twisted slightly as she considered, and her fair skin turned just the slightest shade of pink. "Oh, you know, there are a few things, some for the sake of genetics, some simply because I'd like to like the man. He'd have to be intelligent, gentle, affectionate. It would be nice if he had at least some sense of humor...."

"I think that would be wise...if he's going to get along with you," Gabe agreed, trying to keep the smile from curving his mouth.

Mo's blush deepened and advanced to the roots of her hair. "You're most likely right," she conceded.

Gabe opted not to tease her anymore, but his eyes swept over her from the top of her shining hair, past her lovely lips, her soft breasts, and down the length of those mile-long legs. He took a deep breath. "Anything else? What about looks?"

She shrugged. "Well, I'm not going to lie and say that I'm looking for an ugly man, but it's not as high on my list as some of my other priorities."

Mo looked up at him then, to see how he was taking this, he supposed. He studied her carefully, noting that though she was obviously a little uncomfortable discussing this subject, she never allowed her eyes to waver from his own.

"All right, Mo," he said, deciding to let her off the hook. "Just tell me one more thing. What *does* top your list?"

Her eyes opened wider. She looked to the side, hugging her arms to her, then turned to look him full in the face. "I'd think that would be obvious, Gabriel," she said. "When you ask a man to make a baby with you, the one thing he has to be is...willing."

Mo lifted one delicate shoulder to make her point, and the loose-fitting dress slipped one half-inch farther, exposing the entire pale expanse of her shoulder and a good portion of her chest.

Gabe nodded weakly as he pushed back from the doorframe and finally made his way to his room. Whatever other problems Mo might have, there was one he simply could never imagine: finding a man who was willing. Practically any man in the world would probably lunge at the opportunity to father her baby, to lie with the lady in the dark, her long legs parting beneath him as she waited for his intrusion and his seed. Any man, he thought, swearing softly, remembering the soft, vulnerable look of her when she had kissed the child.

He tore open the remaining buttons on his shirt and tossed it aside as he amended his thoughts. Any man would lunge at the opportunity...except himself.

Gabriel Bonner might well make love, but he definitely did not make babies.

Chapter Three

Housekeeping had always been low on Mo's list of things to do, one of those items she rarely got to and even more rarely worried about. Still, she had agreed to this position, and after getting off to such a horrendous start with Gabriel, she was determined to make amends.

It wasn't his fault she'd spent more time with her fingers glued to a computer keyboard than a broom lately. Or that she'd apparently forgotten even the most basic rules about how to conduct herself in a business relationship with a man.

No, that was her own unique problem, one she intended to remedy immediately. Gabriel Bonner needed a first-rate housekeeper, and he was going to get one. Or, at least, something resembling one. She would definitely see to that.

Thus fired up, Mo climbed into her old Mustang, taking great care not to let the door fall off, and made a quick trip to the library. Armed with an arsenal of books on cleaning, cooking and studies of the male psyche, she figured she was ready for almost anything. Maybe even Gabriel.

The next morning at sunrise, Mo threw on a reasonably modest outfit of jeans and a baggy white T-shirt, made her way to the kitchen and prepared to be the best damn housekeeper the world had ever known.

One hour later, Gabriel found her there.

"Have a seat," she told him, waving a spatula in the air. "Breakfast will be on the table in just a minute."

At the moment, breakfast looked like it was on Mo. Her auburn hair was pulled back and slightly coated in flour. There was egg yolk on the chest of her T-shirt and orange juice on the hem. Even so, she looked enticing. Moreover, the plate of food she placed in front of him smelled unbelievably wonderful, the coffee was a coffee lover's dream of heaven, and the table was perfection, topped with a crisp white cloth and a slender crystal vase bearing a trio of pink rosebuds.

"I filched them from your garden," she confided. "You don't mind, do you?"

"Filch away," he answered, swallowing and smiling up at her. "Come on, have a seat."

Her hands automatically moved to cover the egg stain at her breast. "Oh no, I really couldn't do that," she began, taking a step back. "That's just not the way this is supposed to be done. It says so right here, on page sixty-four." She held a book out for him to peruse. "The hired help does not eat with the residents," she quoted.

Gabe speared another bite of Grecian omelette and grinned up at her. "So now we're going to start worrying about doing everything in a socially correct manner, is that it? Come on, Mo. Sit down."

Still she hesitated, clutching the book to her like a shield. Finally she stuck her chin up in the air. "No, I promised myself last night that I was going to do this right."

"And you are," he agreed. "This is the best damn meal I've had in I don't know when. So join me. Our professional relationship has been anything but conventional so far. I don't see any reason to start now. I don't see that your starving or sitting in some back room alone, or worse, waiting until I'm gone to eat, is going to make a bit of difference."

"What did my aunt do?" she asked suspiciously. "I'll bet she didn't eat with you."

Gabriel rose and pushed her gently into a seat. "Your aunt always had breakfast with 'the ladies'—friends of hers, I believe. Now eat, and when you're done, tell me. Where did someone who seems to have such a minuscule interest in domestic skills ever learn to cook like this?"

"Oh, that." Mo waved his comment away and reached for the sugar bowl as she settled into the chair. "In high school. I was planning on doing an exposé of the home economics department for the student newspaper. You know, how it prepares girls for a life of servitude, how males get favored treatment, that kind of thing. Unfortunately, or fortunately, it didn't work out quite like that. Mrs. Dobbs treated everyone equally unfairly, all the while bellowing that if we were ever going to be independent, single adults, we'd at least need to learn how to feed ourselves. In the end, I lost my enthusiasm for the article. There was nothing to write about."

Mo shrugged, biting into a cinnamon roll. "What's more, I found out that I actually liked to cook. Not that I do much of that anymore. Cooking for one doesn't require much more than a can opener and a microwave. Still . . ." She settled back in the chair, drawing her knees to her chest as she licked a trace of cinnamon from her fingers. "So, how'd you become such an important hardware figure?"

Gabriel dropped his napkin on the table and leaned forward with a slight smile. "Hardware figure?" he asked.

"Oh, I don't know. I inherited the job mostly. But my father made me learn everything from the ground up. And I found I had a feel for the business. I like doing things with my hands."

Mo stopped cold in her perusal of her now clean fingers. She peered out from beneath her lashes with eyes grown bright green with suspicion. "What kinds of things?"

The smile on Gabe's face grew. "Most kinds of things," he said, returning her stare. "But in this case, I like building things, putting things together."

"But you don't do that sort of thing now."

Rising from the table, Gabriel rubbed his jaw with one hand. "No, I don't get out in the field much anymore. But I cruise the stores now and then, just to keep in touch with what the business is really all about. And I still spend a fair amount of time making things as a hobby. This table, for instance," he said, a bit sheepishly.

Letting loose with a squawk, Mo peeled back the cloth that covered it. "You made this? Why didn't you say so? If I'd known—that is, I wouldn't have, I would have—"

"Carved some graffiti in it?" he suggested, unable to suppress the urge to tease her.

"No," she said loudly. "No, I just— I would have treated it more nicely, and I wouldn't have covered it up with a tablecloth—even though this book," she said, snatching up the manual, "said that 'a tablecloth adds a certain polished look.'"

"It does," he agreed, taking the book from her hand and folding her fist inside his own. "Mo," he said softly, "breakfast was fantastic. The tablecloth did add a 'certain polished look.' Everything was perfect. Everything will be fine," he promised once again, knowing that this time, at least, he was saying it for her benefit and, for the moment, anyway, even believing his own words. At least as far as Mo's housekeeping skills were concerned.

He could feel the pulse beating against the delicate skin of her wrist, and when he moved his thumb he stroked...fragile, warm woman.

Mo's lips were parted slightly as she stared at him, wide-eyed and silent.

"I have to get to work now," he told her, clearing his throat. "Thanks for the meal."

She nodded absentmindedly, looking down at where their two hands were joined. "Don't worry," she told him. "I plan to be very busy today."

Gabriel tried not to think about what her comment might mean, remembering how "busy" she'd been yesterday. "More color?" he asked.

"Of course not," she protested. "I think you've had just about all the color you can take. I'll keep a lid on my impulses today."

Gabe was touched by her sincerity and the earnest determination in her eyes. And as he slid his hand away from hers and felt the smooth warmth of her soft skin once again, he swallowed and promised himself that he'd keep a lid on his own impulses, too. He knew how dangerous such things were. And he didn't intend to let anything foolish happen.

It was time to start working longer hours at the office.

The next week Gabriel broke his old record for fevered activity. He worked long hours at the stores, and he took Patrice out to dinner three times. He came home late and tried not to notice the changes that Mo had made in his home—the flowers where there had been no flowers before, the slight scent of roses that pervaded the house, the sparkle where there had merely been clean.

Most of all he tried not to notice that Mo sat up late working at her computer every night. He could almost feel the silent tap of her fingers on the keys as he lay there in the dark, wondering why he'd dropped off Patrice at her home when he'd been inclined to stay and visit in the past, and why he hadn't brought her here when she'd been a frequent visitor in the last few months.

Once when he had stopped to tell Mo that he wouldn't be back for dinner again, he peeked into her room. The place was silent, the keyboard covered, Mo obviously gone while Gabe stood there like a silent intruder in her "home." The shelves, he noted, were cluttered with reference books on every subject imaginable, along with several novels bearing her own name.

Picking one up, Gabe flipped to the front and began to read, then instantly put the book down again. Reading her words awakened a quick need in him to read more, and he didn't want to know that much of her. The variety and number of books she'd both written and read was enough to tell him that Maureen O'Shay was an even more complex creature than he'd suspected. And he found even that too intriguing.

One week later, Gabriel came home to find her perched on top of a ladder, washing a high bank of windows that he was sure Rose always hired someone to clean. She was humming another of her unrecognizable rock numbers as she moved her cloth to the eight-beat count. The ladder was dancing along.

Closing his eyes for a second, Gabe tried to ignore the way Mo's jeans hugged her tight little bottom as he struggled to concentrate on the fact that she was courting disaster. Coming up behind her, he slid his hands up the side of the ladder and stepped onto the bottom rung. His weight halted the motion of the ladder.

Mo swung her head around and stared down to where Gabe stood, his arms trapping her between his body and the ladder. Wasn't it just like the man to show up when she had been trying so desperately to block him out of her consciousness? Now here he was, his breath warm on her middle, so close that if she moved slightly she would brush up against him and feel that warm, dizzying sensation again. The one she had no business feeling. Biting down on her lip, Mo took another step up, turned and sat down on the top of the ladder.

She leaned forward, peering down at Gabriel.

"Hi," she said in a voice that came out much too shaky for her own piece of mind. "Why are you home?"

"I live here," he reminded her with a grin. "Why are *you* dancing around on top of a wobbly ladder?"

"I wasn't dancing," she said, leaning over farther.

Gabe took another step up to steady her and raised a skeptical eyebrow.

Mo frowned. "All right, I was dancing on a ladder. But I didn't realize it. I was simply so involved in what I was doing that I didn't notice the ladder was moving. You don't have to worry, anyway," she said. "I spent a lot of time sitting in trees when I was a girl and I never once fell out. At least, not all the way to the ground. Besides, even if I did fall, I'd never slap you with a lawsuit for something that was my own fault."

A low growl emitted from Gabriel, as he took her hand in his own and backed down the ladder a step. "Come on," he told her. "I'm getting you down from there. How can a woman whose shelves include books on quantum physics and the theory of motion be so uninformed about the dangers of swaying around on a rickety ladder? Come on," he insisted when Mo still remained seated. "Climb off of there or I'm going to pick you up and carry you down myself."

"Hah!" she said, pulling her hand away and clutching the ladder tightly. "Talk about doing something dangerous. Do you know the risks involved in carrying me down this ladder?"

Mo knew what the risks were. Very clearly. There was the risk of being pressed up against Gabriel's warm chest, of feeling his breath on her face, of knowing that his lips were only inches away from her own. And there was no way that she would risk that. She'd rather dance untethered on the top of the Sears Tower than let herself be held in Gabriel's arms.

"Besides," she insisted. "I'm not done washing the windows."

"Mo," Gabe coaxed, rising up two rungs of the ladder. "I'm not a poor man. I can afford to hire people to wash my windows. Men with scaffolding. And common sense," he said hoarsely.

His face was on a direct level with Mo's chest now, and she could tell that he was absolutely aware of it by the way he kept his eyes practically glued to her face. Mo had never been particularly conscious of her individual body parts, but with Gabriel's mouth only a deep breath away, her white, too-tight T-shirt began to feel as if it were shrinking even more and her breasts began to ache in a way that made her want to lean forward and offer their tips up for a kiss. Crossing her arms self-consciously, Mo leaned away as far as she could without doing a backflip off the ladder.

"All right," she conceded. "I can see how upsetting it would be for you to have my blood all over your carpeting. I'll hire a window washer. If you're sure that's what you want."

Gabe let his breath out in a whoosh. He nodded as he moved back down the ladder.

Mo breathed in big gulps of air, relieved that he had removed his disconcerting presence from her immediate vicinity.

"I was just trying to be a good housekeeper," she reasoned as she stood and started to turn.

"You *are* a good housekeeper," Gabriel argued as he braced a steadying hand on the small of Mo's back.

Abruptly she stopped her descent. Her heart was pounding, and she hoped he couldn't feel it. Quickly she moved down and away. "So you're satisfied with me so far? Because Aunt Rose, you know, may be away for weeks, at least until the baby arrives."

Mo was staring at him with a face filled with uncertainty. Gabe marveled at her lack of confidence. She was a woman who wrote for a living, one who already had several books to her credit. And here she was worried about whether he liked the way she did the dishes.

He didn't understand it at all, but for some reason, Mo needed his approval. Was he satisfied with her? Not at all. He'd rather have someone frumpy, someone grouchy, someone who held no appeal for him. But that didn't mean that Mo wasn't good at this job. It wasn't her fault that he felt this damned annoying attraction for her.

Finally he nodded slowly. "I'm satisfied, Mo. Hell, I'll probably have to mess up the place a bit when Rose comes back, or she'll be jealous."

Mo laughed at that. "Not Aunt Rose. She knows she's the best."

But she wasn't, Gabe thought. Mo was unquestionably the best housekeeper he'd ever had. Still, he hoped to hell that Rose would hurry back.

They were both silent, Gabe's hands stilled on the folded ladder, when the phone rang.

Moving quickly, as though the president himself was on the line, Gabe put the ladder aside. "I catch you on that thing when I come back, and I'll personally tie you to a chair and force you to listen to me read all ten chapters of *Safety in the Workplace*."

"Ugh! Sounds boring."

"You ought to know," he told her, quirking up the corner of his mouth. "You own the book. Now stay here until

I get back and we can talk about exactly what your duties are."

Gabe had already picked up the phone when he heard the scraping sound. Stretching the cord, he moved back into the room in time to see Mo wrestling the ladder across the floor.

"Just sit," he barked. "I'll take care of that when I get back. And don't tell me you want to be the best ever," he said, correctly interpreting her guilty look. "I'm your employer and right now I'm ordering you to take a fifteen-minute break. So, sit down."

Mo sat, but she puffed her cheeks out as though she were about to explode.

Satisfied that he had averted another near disaster, Gabe followed the cord back to the hallway and raised the receiver to his ear. "Nora," he said, when he heard the plaintive voice on the other end of the line. "No, I was talking to my new housekeeper. She's got a penchant for bungee jumping off of ladders. I was just a little concerned."

"Well, if you want to feel concerned about something, I can give you someone to worry about," his ex-wife answered.

"Bev," Gabe said with a soft groan and sudden conviction. "Is she all right?"

"Physically?" Gabe could hear Nora's fingernails clicking against the receiver. "She's fine. Otherwise, no. She got her last report card of the year today. Straight C's except for art."

Bev loved to draw and paint. She'd always gotten A's and B's across the board, but then when she was down . . . art would be the only course she could ace without even thinking.

"Give her time, Nora. She needs to adjust. Have you spoken to her, reassured her, offered her your support? Of course you have. We may have our differences, but I know you're a good mother. This sounds so wretched, Nora, but

I wish that other subjects came as easily to her as art. It would make things a hell of a lot simpler for her just now when she's going through so much.''

The clicks got louder. "Gabe, you don't understand. Beverly didn't get an A in art. She failed it. The only subject she enjoys wholeheartedly, and she failed it. It seems she neglected to turn in a number of assignments.''

Silence stretched out before Nora's voice came back on the line. "I don't know what I'm doing anymore, Gabe. I know you hated having me move her away, but the offer to go in with my sister on her shop was too good, and it seemed like Bev was never going to accept the situation—or the fact that you wouldn't be with her all the time—without a little push. Not even two years after the divorce.''

Gabe remembered now why things hadn't worked between him and Nora—besides the lack of emotion. She did love Bev, and she was usually understanding about her daughter's hopes and fears. Except where he was concerned. Nora had always resented the fact that he and Bev were so close, something she'd once admitted in a weak moment. That was the reason, Gabe suspected, whether she even knew it or not, that Nora had moved Bev away, and it was the chief reason he'd known that a custody fight would be ugly. He hadn't wanted Bev to see that kind of ugliness, and so he had let her go.

"She was upset the last time I saw her, Nora, because I hadn't fought you harder about the move. That's most likely a big part of her problem.'' He sighed, letting his head drop forward onto his chest.

"Not all.'' Nora's voice was slightly strangled as she tried for words. "Not all, Gabe. I'm seeing someone now. I think it bothers her.''

Gabe wasn't surprised. Nora was a pretty woman. He wasn't hurt, but he honestly couldn't think of a thing to say, not in the context in which she had offered up this bit of information.

"Gabe?" Nora asked. "Do you think we were wrong? About the divorce?"

"You answer that, Nora. You were the one who asked for it."

"But we didn't love each other."

"No, we didn't."

"We fought." Nora's voice was strained, and Gabe waited in silence, allowing her to finish voicing her thoughts. "Gabe, we would have hurt her, anyway, wouldn't we, fighting the way we did?"

"I'm sure we would have." That much he could answer with a clear conscience. He'd never forget the look of utter terror in Bev's eyes the last time he and Nora had argued.

"But now," Nora went on, "I don't know what to do. I don't think she likes Harry, and I don't know how to make it right this time. She'll get over it, don't you think?"

There was no way Gabe could answer her question. Nora was a grown woman and entitled to go out with the man of her choice. His own concern was for Bev.

"Let me talk to her, Nora. I know she's upset. Maybe I can help. A little, anyway." But deep inside, Gabe cursed the distance that kept him from holding his daughter and comforting her in his arms.

"She's not awake now. After the report card came, she cried herself to sleep. But could you call? Tomorrow?"

"Of course I will."

"And, Gabe? Don't mention the report card, all right? I know it's a lie, but just let her think you called on your own."

"I'll let her tell me herself," he promised. "We'll try to make it right."

With the final click of the receiver, Gabe stood silent for a long moment. Then, with an oath aimed at himself, he slammed his palm down on the table.

Mo found him slumped in a chair next to the telephone table in the hallway. His navy blue tie dangled from his fingertips, dragging on the floor. His shirt had been wrenched open at the throat, and he'd obviously been plowing his fingers through his hair. His eyes, when he finally turned to her, were dark—and angry.

Quickly he straightened, standing as he regained the superior position.

"You're done, then," he said, stating the obvious. "No more aerial acrobatics in the future, Ms. O'Shay, all right?"

His somewhat cool attitude and the fact that he had reverted back to his formal use of her name wasn't lost on Mo. She'd caught him in a moment when his guard was down, and now he was trying to pedal backward, to make her forget what she had seen. The shutters went over his eyes, he straightened his shoulders, and the muscles in his face gradually lost their rigidity.

But for one split second she had seen it, that look inside Gabriel's soul. And she couldn't turn away.

She could ignore the attraction she'd felt for him from the first, for the rough and unfamiliar desire he made her feel. She could ignore those things because she had to, because it would have been emotional suicide to do otherwise. But this she couldn't ignore.

"Gabriel?" she whispered, stepping closer to him. "Something's wrong, isn't it?" She put her hand on his arm where he had rolled up the sleeve, and felt the muscle twitch beneath his skin.

Gabriel put his hand on her own as though to stop her from doing what she had already done. Slowly he drew her hand away and took a deep breath. He stared down into her eyes accusingly. "Practicing amateur psychology on me, are you, Mo?" And she remembered with some guilt the books she'd placed so carelessly on the shelves in her room.

"Don't worry," he assured her, placing his hands on her shoulders. "I'm capable of handling my own problems, and I seem to remember that you're here simply as my employee."

She winced at that, her body tensing. Quickly she pulled back from him. What he said was true and something she'd reminded herself of repeatedly the last few days. But it hurt somewhat to be reminded of the fact when she had only been responding to the need she felt to reach out to him. It hurt, even though rejection was no stranger in her life.

Feeling the shameful heat rising up her face, she gave a slight nod and turned to leave the room.

She was nearing the safety of the door, still managing to keep her shoulders straight. Just a few steps from the doorway, she heard Gabriel call after her.

"Mo. Stop. I'm sorry. That was cruel and uncalled for. I just... Mo, why are you so damn determined to have a child, anyway?"

The sudden change of subject caught her by surprise and sent her swinging round. She knew the answer to his question, told herself that it was simple, uncomplicated. She had love wrapped up in the warmth of her soul... and there'd never been anyone to give it to. Her brothers, born in pairs and many years older than her, had each other; her father had seen in Mo all the flaws of the wife who had so thoughtlessly died, leaving him to raise the children she'd wanted; Aunt Rose had her own family; and Richard, of course, had been a mistake.

But the truth was too demeaning to admit.

"Why does it matter to you?" she asked, evading his question with one of her own. "Why are you asking?"

She raised her chin in stubborn defiance. She could have added that it really wasn't an employer's right to ask such questions, but then, as Gabriel himself had pointed out once before, their relationship wasn't exactly conventional.

"Mo." Gabe's voice dropped to a groan. He moved to her, held out his hands as if to touch her, then lowered them to his sides. "I'm not trying to criticize you. Heaven knows, I've made my own mistakes. And it's obvious from your feelings for your aunt and that little imp you had here last week that you're a caring, kind human being. But a child..." His voice trailed off and he looked away from her. "Damn it, Mo, a child is a big responsibility and so easily hurt. You can't know..."

Mo bit her lip at the anger in Gabriel's voice. She took a deep breath and sighed, uncomfortable with what she was about to say, but intent on saying it, anyway. In spite of his anger, it was clear that what Gabriel needed was... information, on a topic that she understood completely.

"I know," she said solemnly. "I know just how easy it is to hurt a child, any child. And how deep the pain of a ten-year-old girl can be. I'm very much aware of that, you can be sure."

Moving to stand directly before him, she tried to convince him of her sincerity, certain that his concern was somehow tied to his daughter and the phone call. "I was a little girl once. And I know. But," she continued, ignoring the question in his eyes, "I also know the joy a child feels, and that a ten-year-old can be much, much stronger than you think. She can survive a great deal and be happy if she feels in her heart that someone loves her, even a little."

Gabriel's deep blue gaze pinned Mo where she stood. "What you're saying, Mo—why is it that you're so sure?"

"Your Bev knows you love her," Mo said, batting aside his questions. "How could she not, when it's so obvious?"

A tiny smile lifted Gabriel's lips and lightened the darkness of his eyes. "Yes, she does. I'm just not sure that it's enough."

Mo tilted her head, wondering how much to say. "No, probably nothing short of having her father with her twenty-four hours a day could ever be enough, but knowing that you at least *love* her twenty-four hours a day is something tremendously important."

Looking down, Gabriel nodded slightly as he continued to study her. "And you know what you're talking about?"

She hesitated before replying. "Yes, I do," she said, challenging him to doubt her.

It was as if sound and motion stopped for five full seconds. The phone didn't ring. The clock didn't whir. In the canyon of the hallway nothing stirred.

Gabriel shifted his weight.

Mo swallowed hard, the sound suddenly loud in her ears.

He smiled then, slightly, his lips barely tilting up. "Mo..." he said in his smoke-soft husky voice. "Has anyone ever told you what a very good person you are?"

The simple compliment wasn't what caused her heart to jump suddenly, Mo told herself. Nor was it the reverent tone that Gabriel had used, sending shivers up the back of her neck. It was the way he was looking at her, intently, as though he could focus on the core of her that she'd kept carefully hidden until now.

Catching a gasp in her throat, Mo closed her eyes to Gabriel's too discerning gaze. She had only meant to offer solace, not expose herself in such an obvious way.

When she opened her eyes again, Gabriel was studying her, a look of concern in his eyes.

She stared at him, swallowing hard, not really sure what to do. "I . . ." she began. "Thank you. You're very nice, too." She tipped her head back to stare at him earnestly and show him that she meant what she said.

Gabriel's breath came out on a groan. His eyes were dark as he brushed the backs of his knuckles across her lips in a whisper of a caress. "I believe I'm the one who's supposed to be thanking you."

Mo stared up at him, silent, waiting, as he leaned closer, staring deep into her eyes. She reached out as if to touch him back.

And then he moved even nearer, his lips only a second away. "Thank you, Mo. Thank you," he whispered, capturing her mouth with his own.

His lips were gentle, the kiss soft and barely there as he sipped at her. His fingers were warm as he reached to tunnel them through her hair. And the feel of his hands cupping her head, his lips exploring hers was . . . too much.

Mo's mind was spinning. Her legs felt like wobbly building blocks, too delicate to support her weight. And her hands . . . she didn't know what to do with her hands.

She placed them against his chest, fully meaning to push away. But he was warm, his pulse beating against the pads of her fingertips. She tilted her head as Gabriel captured her lips more fully.

With Mo cradled softly against his body, Gabriel felt reality slipping away. Her lips were warm and real and so very sweet. He had only meant to touch her lightly, once. Just once. But now . . . with the silky, violet-scented strands of her hair flowing over his fingers, with her body lightly touching his, her beautiful lips molding to his touch, the pleasure was intense, the need to continue touching her too great to resist.

Shifting her in his arms, he pulled her closer. He breathed in her scent, felt the soft mounds of her breasts against his chest, heard her sweet moan. . . .

His body went rigid, his hands stilled. In the back of his mind a small shred of conscience rose up, demanding to be heard. This wasn't right. Beneath her carefully casual attitude, Gabe had seen something in Mo, something fragile, possibly breakable. And she'd been placed in his care.

She was looking for something he couldn't give. Her life was a tangle of unruly, impetuous emotions and this longing for a child. And his life was as controlled and uncomplicated as he could make it. A hasty, explosive marriage and the bitter taste of divorce and desolate separation had taught him the danger of emotional risks. He didn't take such risks anymore. He didn't get involved. And Gabe didn't intend for that to change.

He couldn't give Mo a child, he couldn't pretend that he would, and he couldn't use her this way. She was in his care and vulnerable. He had to wake up and let her go. But she was lovely and warm and...it was nearly impossible to pull back.

And yet he released her, slowly, letting Mo adjust to the sensation of standing on her own.

"Mo, I—" he began, holding out his hand in a futile gesture. "I'm sorry. I never meant for that to happen."

What excuse could he offer but the truth? Entranced by her concern and the nearness of her soft body... he'd lost his mind temporarily? It was probably better to say nothing.

Mo considered his apology, hugging her arms close as she bent her head and looked down at the toes of her shoes. Long seconds passed. Then she lifted her head in a swish of hair and stared into his eyes. "I don't usually make love to my employers," she whispered.

"We didn't make love, Mo," Gabe corrected. "It was a kiss, only a kiss. If we'd been making love, my mouth would have touched a lot more than just your lips."

Mo sucked in a deep breath. The velvet skin along her jawbone turned to dusky rose.

"It was only a kiss," he repeated in a near whisper. "But you're right. It was a mistake to touch you. Definitely a mistake. I'll try to keep my hands to myself in the future."

Gabriel's matter-of-fact words hit Mo like a ball peen hammer pounding against her self-esteem. She felt naive and embarrassed and angry with herself for breaking her own promise to keep her distance from this man. He wasn't for her. She knew that. She was looking for a man to give her a child and then turn aside, but Gabriel wasn't that man, didn't want to be that man. She'd never ask it of him.... And the alternative, a physical relationship with no hope of a child, was unthinkable. Because already Mo could tell, if Gabriel ever really touched her, if she ever took him deep inside of her, she'd want more, she'd be hurt when it ended. And it *would* end. She and Gabriel had little in common— she couldn't afford to forget that. She wanted no repeats of the past.

The fears and recriminations raced round and round Mo's head as she stood there. She held her face immobile, a technique designed to hide her emotions, one she'd learned as a girl.

"Mo?" Gabriel's voice was laced with worry. Despite his words just seconds earlier, he reached out a hand and touched the side of her face.

Quickly she backed away, gluing on a brilliant smile to disguise the evasive tactic.

"Well then," she said brightly. "I guess I'll just have to cross you off my list of potential genetic donors. Don't worry, though. There's always the mailman. His name was scribbled down right after yours. And with a red asterisk next to it, no less."

"Mo," Gabriel growled. "Don't say things like that."

His gaze was feral. She fiddled with a curl that had come loose, twisting it around her finger as she watched the way her words had affected him. How could she speak as though she considered the conception of a child something to joke about, when she knew that he was worried about his own child right now? She was too rattled, too distraught, to think clearly.

"I'm sorry," she said, amazed at the strangled sound of her voice. "I had no business saying that to you. It wasn't true, anyway. I don't . . . think of you that way."

The silence was thick and heavy.

"Don't berate yourself," he said finally. "I've upset you enough today. It's just that this whole idea of yours—"

"Disgusts you," she supplied in a voice muffled with dread.

"Scares the hell out of me," he corrected. "Absolutely scares the hell out of me. I told you before. Can't you see that there are men who would take advantage of you, use you?"

"You wouldn't. You just told me you wouldn't," she said, looking away as she stared at a thumbnail she had broken earlier in the day. She waited for his words in silence, but they never came.

When she finally raised her head, it was to find Gabriel looking at her with eyes that were fierce. The line of his jaw was tight. "I guess I'll have to keep my eye on the mailman from now on," he said at last, relaxing his face and his stance slightly.

"Why? To warn him I dream of tearing his clothes off?" Mo tried to joke, relieved that Gabriel was finally playing along.

He raised one eyebrow. "You're kidding. Tell me you're kidding. Right now." He reached out and grasped her jaw, imprisoning her.

Mo felt her face heating as he studied her. "I'm kidding," she agreed.

She *was* kidding. And Gabriel would never know that the only man who had drifted into her dreams of late had deep blue eyes and dimples that were usually in hiding. He wouldn't know that he'd stalked her thoughts when she lay asleep, open and helpless, that in those moments his mouth had touched more than her lips. She would never let him know, because he wouldn't welcome those dreams any more than she did. She'd promised herself she wouldn't fantasize anymore, and she meant it. The only place for fantasy in her life was in her books.

"The mailman's safe," she reiterated.

Pulling her chin from Gabriel's grasp, Mo excused herself and fled the room. She took several deep breaths of air, until her hands stopped shaking, her heartbeat slowed and she regained complete control of her thoughts. She treasured that control, held to it tightly. Right up until the moment when she finally lost herself in sleep.

But morning came, as it inevitably does. Mo sat up, pushing back the hair that had fallen into her eyes, rubbing her throbbing temples, staring at the unusually tangled mess of sheets, trying to focus her thoughts on what had awakened her. The alarm wasn't due to go off for another ten minutes.

And then the pounding began again. Gabriel was on the other side of the door, and he was calling her name.

Chapter Four

Throwing on a robe, Mo stumbled to the door and drew it back. She pushed her wayward hair from her face, eyeing the man standing before her. It was early, still dark, but Gabriel was already dressed in a pair of thigh-hugging jeans and a short-sleeved, white knit shirt that clung to the muscles of his chest.

Next to him, Mo felt naked, disheveled. She tried to slide her toes beneath her robe, as she waited for him to speak. A curl slipped into her eyes but she ignored it; her hands were busy clutching together the edges of her robe.

Gabriel reached out and smoothed the curl behind her ear. And Mo noticed that his hands were shaking slightly.

"Mo, I need you," he declared simply.

The words brought a rush of warmth to Mo's sleep-soaked body. She could only stand there, blinking owlishly, hoping she didn't do or say something to give away the tremendous pounding of her heart. Self-consciously she pulled her robe even more tightly about her body, so close that her breasts flattened slightly.

Gabriel closed his eyes.

"Gabriel?" she asked, in her husky early-morning voice.

"Don't worry, I didn't mean that the way it sounded," he assured her, and Mo felt her heart skid, slow down, thudding back into a depressingly sluggish cadence.

"It's Bev," he explained. "Nora just called. She and her new friend, Harry, are taking an unplanned vacation. They want to leave Bev here with me. Will you stay?"

She wrapped her arms about her. "I don't understand."

"Mo," Gabriel explained slowly, "I know that you never wanted to come here in the first place. You only did it for Rose. And I know that Rose never expected you to have to take care of my daughter. This might make you feel differently about staying."

Mo didn't speak as she tried to drink in everything that Gabriel was saying.

"I'm, of course, planning to rearrange my schedule so that I can be here most of the time," he said. "But there may be times—a few—when I might have to be out. Would you— Do you think you could help me? It could be rough at times. Bev's not a happy child right now. She can be difficult, I suppose."

He looked so lost, so concerned, that Mo couldn't help smiling in sympathy.

"Gabriel, it's four in the morning," she reminded him, twisting up one corner of her lips into a smile. "Did you think I'd be easier to persuade if I was extremely groggy?"

Mo's smile widened, and she realized that Gabriel was turning a delicious shade of pink.

"Did you really think I would try to trick you?" he asked, and it was easy to see that he was perturbed.

She rocked back and forth on her toes, thoroughly enjoying herself now that the threat of another mind-robbing physical encounter with Gabriel was over. "Did *you* really think I'd say no?" she countered. "You must know that I'm absolutely delighted that your Bev is coming. Of course I'll stay. How long will she be here?"

Gabriel stared down at her in silence for five full seconds, then a grin split his face. "Have I told you lately what—"

"A very nice person I am? Yes, you have," Mo said, taking a tiny step backward as she remembered what had happened the last time Gabriel had complimented her. "And you still didn't answer my question."

"Two weeks," he declared, still smiling so broadly that his dimples appeared. Really, Mo thought, the man ought to wear a Danger sign.

"It's been a long time since Bev and I have had that long together," he confided. "Thank you for agreeing to stay. And no, I wasn't trying to trick you by getting you up so early. It's just that she's coming tomorrow, and if you wanted to back out, I needed time to find someone—"

"Tomorrow?" Mo shrieked, forgetting herself so completely that she flung her arms out to her sides. The gown dropped open, revealing the T-shirt that skimmed the tops of her exposed thighs.

Gabriel's gaze slid from her face to the worn white fabric that barely hid her chest. He let his eyes linger there, then followed the line of her body to the champagne triangle of satin that showed beneath the edge of the shirt.

His eyes were blue fire, and Mo felt her body beginning to betray her with its response, as though he'd actually slid his hands over her naked skin.

Blushing furiously, Mo grabbed for the edges of her robe, but Gabriel pushed her hands aside, pulling the material firmly around her, then moving back and away.

"Tomorrow," he agreed, his voice low and slightly gritty. "Twenty-eight hours, to be exact."

Mo hoped the pink rush of color was fading from her cheeks. "Then I'd better get going," she said softly, taking another step backward into the room.

"You've changed your mind, then?" Gabriel asked, and the way he looked at her arms clenched around her stomach, Mo knew that he thought he had offended her by staring too closely at her body. She was grateful that he didn't know her breasts ached beneath the thick, fluffy robe.

"Of course not," she assured him. "I meant going to work. There are things I need to do to get ready, and twenty-eight hours isn't a lot of time." But of course, Mo reminded herself, a lot could happen in a little time. In the last day, for example, she had learned a lot: that she couldn't be trusted within an arm's length of Gabriel, that she couldn't even trust herself just looking at him, and that she'd darn well better keep her mind on her work and off the owner of this house.

Mo was very glad that Beverly Bonner would be arriving soon. With his daughter in the house, Gabriel wouldn't continue to give Mo those heated glances. And without those glances, Mo wouldn't be able to shamelessly respond. It was good that she and Gabriel wouldn't be able to explore that attraction anymore. She'd learned too well the foolhardiness of getting involved with a person she had nothing in common with besides attraction.

And by the time Gabriel's daughter went home, her own time would nearly be up, too, Mo reminded herself. Then she'd be back in her own life. Safe.

Getting ready was too gentle an expression for the type of preparations Mo put herself through the next day. She dug out an old toothbrush and cleaned the grout in the bathrooms—all six of them. She polished the brass and aired all the pillows. Armed with a notepad, she made lists of every recipe she could remember liking as a child: pizza, hamburgers, sloppy joes, tacos. She labored over which cookie recipes to use.

"Mo, Bev's only a little girl, not a food critic," Gabriel reminded her as he watched her finish frosting a batch of brownies.

"I know," she agreed. But Mo wasn't knocking herself out just for the lonely little girl that Gabriel had described. She'd seen his face when he spoke of Bev, and she'd watched him today as he'd paced, spending large chunks of time on the phone rearranging schedules, delegating jobs, freeing up his time to be with his daughter.

This visit was an unexpected gift for him, and it touched Mo that his daughter meant so much to him. She hadn't seen the two together yet, but it was obvious that Gabriel's relationship with Bev was elementally different from the one she'd had with her own father.

She wanted this time to be special for him and his child. And, she admitted, to be special, vicariously, for herself.

"Are you complaining about my preparations?" she teased, holding a brownie beneath his nose. "Admit it. You liked the spaghetti I made you for lunch."

He leaned back in his chair, closing his eyes as he tried to ignore the treat she had pulled back out of his grasp. "I adored your spaghetti, I have dreams of the lasagna you made last week, and your brownies—" he suddenly lunged forward and grabbed the crumbling square from her hand "—they're pure paradise."

"Humph!" Mo smiled smugly, leaning toward him, her crumb-filled hand held aloft. "For a man who doesn't eat Oreos, you certainly know your chocolate. I knew you couldn't resist. At least, not for long." She punctuated her declaration by licking the crumbs from her fingers.

Looking up, she saw that Gabriel's eyes had grown darker, the brownie forgotten as he watched the movements of her tongue.

She froze, her lips poised next to her last finger, the small one, and Gabriel grasped her wrist, tugging her hand toward him. With her finger resting against his lips, he spoke, the sound sending vibrations through her skin. "You're right," he rasped, still holding her to him. "I can't resist for long. But I'm trying." And in one slow movement, he ran his tongue over the fleshy pad of her finger, then released her. "I'm trying, Mo," he repeated as he stood and left the room.

Mo cupped her hand in the other for long, long minutes, clasping both to her chest, trying to still her erratic heartbeat. Then, moving on shaky legs, she began to clear the table.

Gabriel's meaning was perfectly clear to her. She was a woman playing with matches and in grave danger of starting a forest fire. Forest fires were a phenomenon she'd studied at one point in her life. She knew how unpredictable they were—often unstoppable, the fire storm of flame and ash could leave a trail of scars and wounds that were slow to mend. She couldn't let her guard down and tease when Gabriel was around, because when the two of them were together, the smoke of physical attraction always seemed to hang in the air. And that was nothing to fool around with.

The rest of the day passed in a slow haze for Mo. Gabriel was gone, and yet she was aware that he'd be back, bringing with him that magnetic presence she didn't know how to deal with. All day she waited, working, afraid to let down her guard.

Dinner came and went.

At ten she dropped into bed, but she didn't sleep. She was too aware of Gabriel's absence and knew that she herself had brought it on with her foolish teasing. Gabriel didn't like the fact that he wanted her. She didn't want to want him, either. And she didn't want him to think that she was trying to start anything.

Finally, she heard his steps on the stairs. He went past her room, not even hesitating. Then she heard his door close.

The darkness of the night closed in around her. She could sense Gabriel's nearness, knew that he was sleeping. It disturbed her how much the man was getting to her.

This attraction to Gabriel wasn't what she was after, at all. What she wanted was a simple, uncomplicated coupling with a safe stranger that would end in a baby. Gabriel wasn't that stranger. He had nothing to offer her, and she had nothing that he wanted—at least, not in a permanent sense.

But when they got close... It was too frightening to think of, this desire for the man.

Suddenly the huge house was too small, Gabriel's room at the end of the hall was too close, his sleeping form was too appealing for her to stay in this house one more minute tonight. Tomorrow would be different. Tomorrow Bev would be here. But for now...

Mo threw off the covers and pulled on jeans and a ragged blue sweatshirt, then tiptoed out of her inky room and down the hall. The stairs were tricky in the dark, but she made it, only tripping slightly on the bottom step.

She bumped her hip on the telephone table in the hallway, but slipped past it soundlessly. She could feel Gabriel in the air, smell him, taste him. And she had to be away before she did something too foolish to even consider.

Hurrying to the door, she found she'd waited too long. The light flipped on, and he stood there, poised at the top of the stairs, shirtless, staring down at her like some fierce warrior.

"Where the hell are you going?" he demanded, as he began to descend the stairs.

As he drew near, she swallowed, watching the play of muscles across his torso as he moved.

"I—I—" In truth, Mo wasn't sure. "Out." It was all she knew to say. It was all she actually knew.

Gabriel had almost reached the bottom of the steps now, and Mo had to look up as he came closer. She was incredibly conscious of the bare expanse of his chest and of her own heart pumping away.

"Mo," he reasoned, in that strong, soothing voice she'd grown to know. "It's three in the morning. Go back to bed."

She stood staring up at him, challenging his right to tell her what to do on her own time. And he had the nerve to lift his lips in a smile.

Gabe rested one hand high on the doorframe behind her. She breathed in the scent of him as he studied her, then brushed the knuckles of his other hand gently across her cheek.

Mo sucked in her breath in a small gasp.

"Why are you so damn lovely?" he whispered.

Slowly he leaned over her, his mouth descending.

It was all she could do to keep breathing, to keep from standing on her toes so that his lips would reach hers more quickly. She wanted to curl her arm around his neck and pull him to her. She wanted to place her hands against his chest and twine her fingers in the soft curls that angled down into his jeans.

As he neared her, she licked her lips, she closed her eyes, she took a breath. Her body swayed toward his as if she couldn't help herself.

"No," she suddenly said. She wanted this and yet she didn't. Closing her eyes, she forced herself to remember Richard and how foolishly she'd behaved, reaching for something that had never really existed. She had promised herself not to go through that again. She wanted more than just kisses and caresses in the dark. Or she wanted nothing, which was better than throwing her heart at a man and having it stepped on . . . or worse, ignored.

Gabriel paused, breathing in the sweet scent of Mo as his lips hovered near hers. She was so tempting, so beautiful, so desirable. He swallowed hard, staring at her full lower lip. It was luscious . . . and it was trembling.

"No," she whispered again, shaking her head, her eyes wide and pleading.

He breathed in deeply, then let the air out, pushing himself off the wall. "No," he agreed.

The silence enclosed them as he tried to bring his breathing back to normal. There was something that seemed to draw him and this woman together every time they met, and he knew she was fighting it just as hard as he was. It was a good thing that one of them had been thinking straight tonight. He would have had her pressed tightly against him in only a moment. He would have been running his hands over every curve that he'd been longing to touch. The thought made him burn, made him shake.

Breathing out again, Gabe ran one hand along his jaw. "Mo, I didn't really come down here to—to take advantage of you. I just came to tell you I was sorry about this afternoon. It's not your fault that I want you."

She bit her lip, staring up at him solemnly. "I think today that it was," she said, shaking her head. "I wasn't thinking about what I was doing. But I'll be smarter next time."

God, Gabe thought, he hoped so. He hoped they'd both be a hell of a lot smarter. Because so far they were doing everything wrong. So far they were aiming for the kind of disaster he'd initiated once before when he'd lost control of his senses.

Thank goodness Bev would be here tomorrow.

* * *

A whoop of girlish laughter woke Mo the next morning. She lay there staring at the ceiling, listening to her heartbeat as she waited for another sound.

A giggle followed.

It was the day.

Gabe's daughter had arrived, and Mo still lay dressed in the wrinkled blue sweatshirt she'd worn when she'd fallen into bed the night before.

"Oh damn," she declared. What a mess she was. "Damn, damn, double damn." Then for good measure, "Triple damn," as she rolled out of bed and began digging through her closet. White denims. A kelly-green blouse. It would have to do.

She couldn't find her shoes and finally gave up altogether, feeling the crush of the thick carpeting beneath her socks as she made her way down the stairs.

Gabe was there, talking to his daughter, his arms crossed in a languid pose, a huge grin on his face.

Before her, Mo saw a petite little ballerina of a girl, the dark, glossy curls at the back of her head swaying as she talked and laughed, using her hands for emphasis.

"Daddy," she said, suddenly stopping in the midst of her story. "Are you going to bring in my stuff? I made you something in art class. You're gonna love it. It's so-o-o neat."

"Well, then I guess I better bring in your stuff, cupcake, hadn't I?"

"Yes, please." The little girl was practically dancing on her toes. "I can't wait. I can't wait. I can't tell you. But I've got to tell you. It's an ashtray. And I know you don't smoke, but everybody had to make something out of clay and my pot fell apart, so I made an ashtray. And not one like all the other kids did, either. Mine's different. And I had to pack it very carefully so it wouldn't break in my suitcase, because it's got legs. And arms and a head, too. I know you're going to like it."

Gabriel raised one brow and smiled at the little girl, reaching out to tweak her nose. "You're a nut. You know that?"

"A nice nut?" She giggled as she said it, and Gabe smiled in return, the way people do when they share old jokes.

"A very nice nut," he agreed. "The nicest."

He was looking at the child as though she had descended from the heavens, and suddenly Mo knew that she couldn't walk into the midst of this. It was a private moment, two people who'd been separated against their wills. They needed time alone to get to know each other again.

Slipping backward, Mo began to retrace her steps.

She was stopped by the sound of Gabriel clearing his throat. "Bev, I'd like you to meet Mo. She's taking Rose's place for a while, and she's the person who put the pink flamingos on the lawn. Maybe you'd like to tell her how much you liked them."

Bev turned in a small pirouette, a slight grin on her face, which froze when she looked at Mo.

Mo held out her hand. "I've been looking forward to meeting you, Bev," she said with a smile. "I hear you're quite an artist."

Bev suddenly looked down, studying the toe of her shoe. "I draw a little," she mumbled. "That's all." At a nudge from Gabriel, she looked up at him. "The flamingos were okay," she added quietly.

Mo glanced up, noting the frown on Gabriel's face, and gave a slight shake of her head. "I'll just go get breakfast ready," she told them, as she backed out of the room and slipped into the silence of the kitchen.

She dug flour out of a canister, mixing in eggs and milk, wondering at the scene she'd just witnessed. The enthusiasm on Bev Bonner's face had disappeared like the sun dropping over the horizon. Mo wondered if the little girl was just shy. It wasn't all that unusual in a child.

Pouring batter onto a griddle in generous dollops, Mo gave a little shrug. This was going to be a good day. The sun was shining, the flowers were blooming, Gabriel was smiling, and there were pancakes loaded with fat blueberries cooking on the stove.

The door flew open behind her. Mo turned just in time to see Bev plop herself down in a chair.

"Dad said I should come eat. He's fixing the fastener on my suitcase," she said in a low and expressionless voice.

Mo pasted on a smile. "I understand your dad's very good at fixing things."

Beverly's face remained blank and unsmiling, though her blue eyes revealed more than she knew. She took the plate of food that Mo placed before her and stared at it as though it were poison.

It was obvious that the little girl wished that Mo would leave. Mo considered doing just that, then stopped. The two of them would have to be together from time to time for the next two weeks. The situation wasn't going to work if she left every time Bev came into the room.

"Well," Mo said, feeling like she had the first time someone had pitched her in the water before she learned to swim, "you'll be here a whole two weeks. I'll bet you and your dad have lots of things planned."

Bev's mouth twisted slightly, as though she were going to cry. "Two weeks isn't so much," she finally managed.

"No," Mo said quietly. "I know it isn't. But it can be a good two weeks if you let it. Or," she added, "you can spend your time worrying about the end and waste all the fun."

A silent stare was all the answer Mo received.

"I have to go to my room," Bev said, standing suddenly. "I've got stuff to do. And I'm not really hungry."

"All right," Mo agreed, not wanting to push the issue of breakfast. "When I see your father I'll tell him that you're getting reacquainted with your animals."

Bev was making a beeline for the door. She stopped just inside. "Harry says I'm too old for stuffed animals."

"Harry?"

The little girl nodded tersely. "Harry's a salesman. One day he came to help my mom set up an exercise bike, and now he's always at my house."

This sudden revelation hung in the air between the sullen child and Mo. It was all too obvious what she was getting at. And for all her churlish ways, it was also clear that this was a child who had some serious pain and needed whatever comfort she could get, even if it was only hugging a familiar old friend made of cotton and batting.

Mo nodded. "Well, I'm sorry Harry feels that way about stuffed animals, but I don't think your dad feels you're too old. He asked me to put a new ribbon around your poodle's neck just yesterday. It might hurt his feelings if you packed your animals away so soon after that."

Quickly Mo forgave herself for the small lie. She would talk to Gabriel, and Bev need never know that she herself had chosen to replace the frayed and wrinkled blue grosgrain with a soft length of fresh satin.

"I'll wait, then," Bev agreed softly. Again she turned to go.

"Bev." Mo stopped her with a word. The little girl didn't turn around.

"I'm not Harry, Bev," Mo told her. "In the first place, I couldn't set up an exercise bike if my life depended on it. Not without a few hundred manuals."

Her attempt at humor fell on silence.

"And in the second place," she rushed on, "I'm just here to take care of the house. And only for a very short time. I won't be hanging around forever. You don't have to worry."

For a minute, Mo thought that Bev was going to turn around and speak. Then the girl straightened her shoulders and gave one quick nod without turning. "Thank you for the food," she said, leaving the room.

The day passed slowly for Mo. She stayed in the kitchen, not even coming out for lunch, ignoring Gabriel's request that she join him and his daughter out on the picnic table.

"Work to do," she'd told him, rushing back to her spot at the sink.

But she couldn't put him off when dinner had been served and eaten and she was still shuffling around the kitchen. The kitchen door swung back, and Gabriel was standing there, watching her.

Mo buried her arms to the elbow in dishwater even though she'd already washed the last plate.

"I have a dishwasher," he suggested gently.

"I'm old-fashioned," she said, lifting her chin.

"You?" His incredulous tone brought her head up and she saw his smile. "Not a chance, Mo. You're not old-fashioned. You're hiding. I want to know why. And don't worry that Bev is listening outside the door. She's upstairs getting reacquainted with her 'stuff,' as she calls it. So spit it out. What's wrong?"

"Nothing's wrong. What could be wrong?"

"I don't know, but I have an awfully strong feeling it has something to do with my daughter."

"No," Mo said, shaking her head. "It's not Bev. It's Harry. She thinks I'm like Harry. She's worried that I'll move in and take over, change her life with you."

"I see," Gabe said, turning her around to face him. He took a cloth and moved it gently down her arms, wiping away the damp suds. "I do see," he agreed when Mo made a frustrated movement and started to step away.

"What exactly did you tell her?" he continued.

Mo looked up at him, swallowing hard, crossing her arms in front of her tightly when he dropped the cloth. "Me? Well, I told her the truth. I told her that she had nothing at all to worry about, that you and I were only business associates and that I'd be gone soon. I told her that there could never, ever be anything between you and me."

The silence went on so long that Mo wondered if Gabriel had heard her.

"That's what you told her?" he finally asked.

"She needed reassurance," Mo explained.

"So you told her that you and I were simply business associates." Gabriel's eyes were fierce, brightly blue and... very attentive.

Mo raised her chin. "It was the truth," she said softly.

Gabriel reached out. He cupped her chin, running his thumb softly over her lips. His touch made a shiver run through her.

Slowly, deliberately, he moved his hand lower, brushing at the pulse point in the hollow of her throat, sliding his hand over the slope of her breast, barely touching the crest with his thumb.

Mo swallowed her gasp, but she couldn't slow her heartbeat or hide the way her nipple hardened at his touch.

"The truth, Mo," Gabriel said in a husky whisper, taking her hand and placing it over his own thrusting heart, "is that if you believe that you and I are merely business associates, then you've been wearing blinders ever since the day you arrived. But you are right about one thing. Nothing can happen if we don't let it."

"And we won't let anything happen," Mo said with more conviction than she actually felt.

"No, we won't," he agreed. "At least, not much. I don't want my daughter to be frightened, Mo, but I certainly don't want her to spend her life hiding from the truth, either. The real truth," he emphasized.

And then he was gone, leaving Mo to wonder what he had meant by "not much." Somehow she knew she was going to have another restless night. And it was all Gabriel Bonner's fault.

Chapter Five

Gabriel looked down at the blank sheet of paper on his desk. He'd been trying to work for hours, without any results. Something was interfering with his concentration... and he knew exactly what it was.

It was Mo. Ever since he'd had that talk with her about Bev, she'd been avoiding him. Completely.

"Almost completely," he muttered, sliding his fist across the polished oak desk top. She hadn't shown her face, but her touch had been evident in every outing he'd gone on with his daughter. There were the newly shined bikes that he and Bev had ridden along the lake, the bottle of sunscreen and the lunch that had been packed when they'd gone to the beach, the rain gear that had been set out when they'd hit the ballpark on an ominously cloudy day. It was clear that Mo was taking care of him and Bev, making sure that they had plenty of uninterrupted time together.

But it was also compellingly clear that Bev still tensed up every time Mo walked into the room.

And that Mo obliged his daughter by trying to make herself scarce as much as possible. It had been three whole days since he'd really seen her.

Gabriel ran his hand along the curve of his jaw, wondering what he could do to make Mo see the truth. He and Bev couldn't live in a terrarium, separated by glass from the rest of the world. This whole scenario wasn't healthy for Bev, and it was anything but fair to Mo.

If she had seemed alone when he first met her, it was nothing compared to what she was like now. She moved like a silken shadow, trying to keep from intruding on his privacy with his daughter, trying to make herself fade away.

Gabe allowed himself a small smile at that. Mo probably thought she'd kept completely out of view for the last few days. As if he wasn't aware of her. Constantly.

"Damn." Even admitting that made him squirm against the leather of his chair. It wasn't right that he should be spending so much time thinking about Mo, listening for her step, wanting to feel her lips against his own. It had to stop. Sometimes he felt like he could burn up just by standing too long in the light that she shed, and all that would be left of him and the people around him would be ashes.

He didn't want to feel that way. He didn't want a relationship where that much emotion was at stake. He wanted to walk away and pretend she didn't exist. But he couldn't. Because, like it or not, Mo mattered. And he wasn't going to let her play the part of the invisible woman out of some misguided concern for Bev. He had to do something.

And while he was doing it, he was just going to have to control himself. If he could.

Abruptly, Gabe stood and left the study. He knew where to find her. She'd seemed unusually preoccupied with the laundry room of late. Too preoccupied. She'd washed clothes he didn't even know he had, like his old high school football jersey. And the stretched-out summer-camp T-shirt he'd worn when he was a counselor... about a billion years ago. Mo was obviously running low on laundry. It was time to make his move.

Continuing through the house, he rounded the corner and stepped silently through the open door of the laundry room.

She was there, just as he'd thought. Her slim body was curved over the washing machine, her elbows resting on the white metal, a book open wide on the lid. Slender fingers ribboned a path through the fiery tendrils of her hair, and her lushly curved little bottom stuck out in a very prominent and inviting way.

Gabe folded his arms across his chest to prevent himself from doing something foolish—like spanning her waist with his hands, pulling her back against him, touching her....

"What are you reading?" he whispered hoarsely.

Mo let out a tiny gasp, raising up and turning so fast that the book slid off the machine.

She stared at him, wide-eyed, her breath coming just a bit too fast.

"It's a... a stain-removal guide," she managed, bending to quickly pick up the book.

But not quickly enough. Gabriel quirked up one eyebrow.

"You read those for fun, do you? The way you were so totally engrossed, I would have sworn it was something more interesting."

Mo waved one hand in the air. "Well, after all, it's...my job. It's—"

"A manual on child psychology?" he offered.

Turning a delicious shade of rose, Mo lifted her hands in a slight gesture that admitted her guilt.

"I just thought it might help," she explained. "I thought I knew everything there was to know about children. But that's obviously not true, and—"

"Don't," he said, stopping her with one word. "It's not your fault, Mo, that my daughter is so cautious. If it's anyone's fault, it's mine. Mine and Nora's. Because... although she's just ten, Bev is more... she's more like a little adult than a child. We did that to her, Nora and I, with our carelessness, and the circumstance of our marriage. You can't blame yourself because she's suspicious of you."

Mo sucked in her lip, her questions in her eyes, though she didn't say a word.

Sighing, Gabe reached out and traced the frown lines on her forehead with two fingers.

"My wife and I didn't have much of a marriage, Mo. Not really. Bev was conceived— Well, let's just say that when my family died, I wasn't myself for a long while. Bev was conceived at a party on a night when I'd had too much to drink. Nora and I got married with good intentions, but for all the wrong reasons. Things like that don't slide past a child. As much as we both loved her, we couldn't pretend that our love extended to each other. And then, with the divorce, with the move, Bev lost a great deal of her security. She grew up too fast."

Mo closed the book, stood up straight and pressed her shoulders back in a determined gesture. "Maybe that's true, Gabriel. You know your daughter best, and you might be right. But even if she's had to grow up faster than most children, there's still a little girl inside there somewhere. I saw her that day when she first arrived, when she was talking to you before she noticed me. She's absolutely thrilled to be here with you. It's just me she's afraid of. I'm the one making her skittish. And I don't know how to change that."

Gabriel studied her for a moment and saw genuine concern shadowing her eyes.

"I might know how," he said with a small attempt at a smile. Taking her hand, he pulled her toward the door of the cramped room. "Bev may be suspicious of you, but she's also very human. And curious. If you want her to like you, she's got to get to know you. As in face-to-face contact," he emphasized.

When he stopped to look at Mo and see how she was reacting to his suggestion, she wasn't smiling. Not at all. But she hadn't put the brakes on her sneakers yet, either.

"And," he continued, "she can't get to know you or like you if you're spending all your time hovering between the bottles of laundry detergent, can she?" He looked over his shoulder, frowning at the washing machine as though it had criminal intentions.

Mo's answer to his question was silence, three long seconds of silence. Then she pulled free, stopping in her tracks, her feet spread wide. "Why would it matter to you how Bev feels about me when you know I'll be gone soon, anyway?"

Gabe paused, considering her question, his answer. What could he say? That at times he saw more of a child in Mo than in Bev, that he thought she'd be good for his daughter? Or that even though he couldn't explain why, he wanted Mo to feel good about being here with him, and he thought friendship with Bev might help. Both were true, but...

"I just want her to be a happy little girl who doesn't worry unnecessarily," he said, choosing a third truth. "If she lives her life like this with both me *and* her mother, that's a problem. A serious one. What would happen if one of us decided to get married again? I want Bev to learn that her mother and I will love her no matter what, no matter who else comes into our lives."

Mo looked at him solemnly, slowly digesting all he'd said. Then she nodded. It wasn't much of a nod, but it was a small concession. "All right, I'll try, then. Maybe you're right. Maybe she just needs to see that I'm no threat to her, to see that you and I are just business—"

She stopped at the warning light in his eyes.

"Just friends," she amended. "That could help. If she sees more of me, she'll know that she needn't worry, that I couldn't possibly be like Harry, a man who ridiculed her for having a few stuffed animals." Mo's wrinkled nose told Gabe clearly what she thought of Harry's opinion.

Smiling, Gabriel chose to ignore Mo's insistence on sticking to the word *friends*. "Yes, she'll know that you're not like Harry," he agreed. "The man has a beard that hangs down to his chest. I'm betting Bev will see the difference between you and Harry right away, once she finally gets a decent look at your face."

Mo gave him a punch on the arm. "You know what I mean."

"I know," he agreed solemnly. "And I'm glad that you've decided to come out of the detention room." He gestured toward the now-vacant laundry room.

"No more hiding. Please," he said. "You'll eat with us from now on?"

She shrugged her acceptance.

"And go on an outing or two?" he cajoled. At her frown, he tilted his head. "Mo," he drawled, "don't get cold feet on me now."

"One outing," she agreed. "Then we'll see."

"Good," he said with a wide grin. "I've got something really special planned for later in the week."

Two days passed, and Mo still didn't know what Gabriel's big plans were. She took her meals with Bev and Gabriel, and the two adults talked, their conversation too animated as they tried to pull Bev into discussion after discussion, and ultimately failed. The little girl's big-eyed solemn stares noticed everything, and Mo began to feel like passing the green beans to Gabriel was an act of seduction. Sometimes it felt like the truth, when her fingers accidentally brushed against his, and she felt that now-familiar tingle go slithering up her arm.

She was starting to think that she would never learn to control her senses around Gabriel. And she was starting to think that things would never change as far as Bev was concerned, that the little girl's hurts and fears were too deep, that Harry must have been more of a jerk than anyone could guess.

And then Gabriel slipped into the kitchen one Thursday morning.

"It's the big day," he announced in a theatrical whisper, grabbing an apron from her fingers and taking her by the hand. "Leave the house, the laundry, the dishes, whatever other wonderfully stupendous tasks you had planned for today. Bev and I are taking you out on the town. We're stealing you away, forcing you to do our bidding. In short, I'm kidnapping you, Mo. Now, are you going to come along peaceably or am I going to have to put this apron to use and tie you up?"

She leaned back, watching the wicked rise of his brows as he held out the dangling apron strings and took one of her wrists in his hand, a look of mock concern on his face.

Pulling her hand away, Mo crossed her arms over her chest, giving him her best you've-got-to-be-kidding look.

"Okay, you're right. Trussing up a woman is not exactly my style," he conceded. "I'd be much more likely to simply toss you into my arms and carry you out to the car if I had to."

Mo smiled, ignoring her heated blush as she took the apron from him and tossed it on the counter. "Well, I guess you're lucky, then, that I'm not going to put up a struggle. I surrender. I'm yours for the day."

Looking into her eyes, Gabriel stepped closer, suddenly serious. "Good." He touched the curve of her cheek with one fingertip. "I was half-afraid you'd bolt and run or go hide in the laundry room again. And I really wouldn't have forced you into something you don't want, you know.''

''I know. Lugging an irate woman to your car isn't really your style, either. I'm not surprised that you're relieved that I'm so willing,'' she teased.

Bad choice of words, she told herself, sensing Gabriel's hesitation.

But if he read more into her words than she had intended, Gabriel chose not to comment.

''This day will be good for all of us, Mo—you'll see'' was his only response.

Mo wasn't so sure about the ''good for all of us'' part. She never really trusted her emotions when she had to be around Gabriel for more than five minutes. Bev was still holding back, her little face too often taut and drawn. But Mo didn't know what else to do. So, with only a slight hesitation, she agreed to Gabriel's plans. ''All right, where are we going? Do I need to change?''

He studied her short khaki jumpsuit. ''No, what you're wearing is great. Just the right amount of casual.''

''For what?''

He raised his brows and pasted on a grin. ''For the amusement park. Bev's always had a thing about them.''

For just a moment, Mo considered backing down. She felt a wave of something resembling impending doom. But she tamped it down. Nothing was going to happen if she didn't let it. So she forced out a nod and stepped past Gabriel. ''That's fine. I've always had a thing about amusement parks, too.''

It was true. Mo did love amusement parks. She adored them. She was addicted to the thrill of the rides, of having her stomach drop out from beneath her. She coveted the feel of the wind whisking past her face and the sky sailing past at a breakneck speed.

There was only one problem.

At some point during the day, her body might decide to declare war on itself. It always had in the past.

That's all right, that was years ago. This time I'll watch myself. I'll keep things under control, Mo promised herself as she slid into the back seat of Gabriel's big white car.

Gabriel opened his mouth to suggest that there was room in the front with him and Bev, Mo was sure. But she shook her head. She wasn't going to force herself onto the little girl's personal space. She would take things as slowly as Bev needed to.

"So, when was the last time you were on a roller coaster, Mo?" Gabriel asked, trying to include her in the quiet conversation that was taking place in the front seat.

"Oh, a while. I don't really remember," she said breezily.

Years, her stomach reminded her. It remembered perfectly. And why she hadn't been on one since.

"How about you? Do you have a favorite ride, Bev?" Mo ventured, trying to ease into the conversation.

The little girl turned in her seat, her dark braid twisting behind her. She studied the question quietly, then tipped her head. "Well, I like the really fast ones, the ones that turn you upside down and all around. Those are the best. Especially the roller coasters."

"I remember," Mo agreed with enthusiasm. She could already almost feel that terrifying dizzying sensation that was so much fun, because you knew that you were safe, that you wouldn't really fall.

Don't do it, her stomach ordered.

She wrinkled her nose and gave her stomach a comforting pat. Bev had shared an entire sentence with her. And Gabriel was smiling, his window rolled down, the wind teasing his dark hair. His suddenly evident dimples told her that he was looking forward to the next few hours.

She rolled her own window down and treated herself to the breeze.

It was going to be a good day, Mo told herself with a smile. Nothing was going to keep her from enjoying it. Nothing.

Two hours later, Mo wasn't so sure.

In spite of the fact that Bev had opened up for one brief second, the little girl was now subdued, tense.

Bev was watching Gabriel. She was watching *her*, Mo knew, gauging their reactions to each other, looking for something that would show her that she was safe.

And Mo was determined to give it to her.

Ruthlessly, Mo pulled her thoughts from Gabriel every time he looked at her, every time he smiled, laughed. Her eyes, her whole body, wanted to turn to him and share the moment, to reach out and touch him, to laugh up into his eyes.

But she wouldn't let that happen, no matter how painful it was to hold herself in check. Because she didn't do those kinds of foolish things anymore, and because Bev would see, would think the wrong things . . . that she and Gabriel were more than just friends, when, of course, that was all they could ever be.

Instead, Mo watched herself. Her smiles were all for Bev.

And Bev clung to her father's side as though he'd disappear soon. Mo supposed he would. In just a few short days.

The thought spurred her on, made her more determined to break through the fence that Bev was trying so hard to maintain. If she could offer Bev a shred of friendship to latch on to, the child might not spend so much time thinking about how quickly her visit would end.

"Come on—do you like to get wet?" Mo asked suddenly, looking down at Bev, touching her arm inadvertently. She pointed across the grounds. "Look, let's ride the log slide. How about it?"

For maybe two seconds, Bev was caught off guard. Her eyes glowed with the thrill of trying something new. She started off in the direction Mo had indicated. Then she turned back around. "Your clothes will get soaked," she explained quietly, coming to a complete stop. "It'll be messy."

"I know," Mo said with a conspiratorial smile. "That's why we're doing it."

Bev looked at her suspiciously. "Grown-ups don't always like messy stuff."

"Grown-ups?" Mo asked, beginning to get the picture.

"Harry doesn't," Bev explained.

Mo was beginning to hate even the sound of the man's name. "Do I look like Harry?" she asked indignantly. "I don't think so. And *I* can't wait to get splashed on a hot day like this. Come on, who are you trying to save—me or yourself?"

Bev's face took on a determined look. She pressed her lips together, taking up the challenge as she raced ahead.

Gabriel came up behind Mo, stilling her own forward momentum. "Are you really that eager to get soaked or are you just being nice for Bev's sake?" he whispered near the nape of her neck. His breath caressed her skin.

Mo shivered slightly. She whirled away from Gabriel's lips, the tang of his cologne that drifted near and the sense that if she stepped back one little bit, she'd be in his arms.

"I'm absolutely true-blue," she declared, turning and trying to look offended. "But I can see you're hanging back. Maybe you're the one who's just like Harry."

"Do I look like Harry?" he asked indignantly, repeating her words.

"Hmm. Having never seen Harry, I can't say for sure," she reminded him. "But I guess you can't have that much in common with him. I hear he has a truly impressive beard." She eyed the clean, chiseled line of Gabriel's jaw.

"*And* I happen to like messy stuff," he reminded her, leaning near with a grin.

Taking in a deep breath, Mo cast a glance over her shoulder. "Bev—" she began.

"Is staring right at us, Mo," he told her. "So stop acting as though we're doing something wrong. You've been avoiding me and giving me guilty looks all day. And I want you to stop it. Now. Bev needs to know that her father can have . . . friends, without it being any threat to her."

"Is that why you were breathing down my neck a few seconds ago?" Mo asked nervously. "To show Bev what good friends we are?"

Gabe laughed out loud at that, but he held his hands palm up, admitting his guilt.

"No," he said, turning serious. "I was contemplating kissing your lovely neck, because sometimes when I look at you, my body reacts so strongly to yours that I forget that it wouldn't be smart to . . . touch," he said softly. "I find myself wanting to try to coax you into my bed. I think you know that. But that's—well, I guess that's not the point at the moment.

"The point is that my daughter *does* need to know that I can be near you and still love her just as much as I ever have. I don't know what's going on with Nora and Harry, but someone is sending the wrong messages to Bev. I'm not going to let that happen here. I don't want her to live in fear. So, come on. Bev's holding our place in line, and if I know my daughter, that little foot is going to be stamping if we make her miss getting on this time."

Mo stood there staring, wide-eyed. She'd almost forgotten to breathe during parts of Gabriel's speech. Now she slowly nodded and simply followed him.

Bev was looking slightly disgruntled when Mo and Gabriel made their way to where the little girl was standing. "What were you doing?" she asked bluntly.

"We were talking, Bev," Gabriel answered.

"He wasn't sure about this ride," Mo confided a little more enthusiastically than was necessary. She wasn't just afraid that Bev might have seen Gabriel's lips against her skin—she was also afraid that she wasn't hiding her own reactions to Gabriel's nearness very well, from Bev...or from Gabriel. "I had to twist his arm," Mo continued. "Can't have him spoiling our fun."

Bev raised her brows at that.

"Hey, I wasn't chickening out," Gabriel protested, agreeing to the game.

Mo looked down her nose in mock disbelief. "That's all right, you don't have to save face with your daughter. She won't hold your cowardice against you, will you, Bev?"

Bev raised her brows higher and shook her head. "Of course not, Daddy. You can sit in the middle if you don't want to get so wet. Can't he?" she asked, peering up at Mo.

"Definitely," Mo said, relaxing a bit for the first time. For once Bev was too caught up in the moment to avoid speaking to her. "Definitely."

For the next hour the obliging rays of the sun warmed them, just as Mo's heart was being warmed by the rare chance to share something so special as a simple afternoon outing with this man and his child. True, Bev hadn't made any overtures and only spoke when spoken to, but at least she wasn't cringing whenever Mo came near.

Mo liked the way Gabriel included his daughter in their conversations, not pretending she wasn't there the way some adults would have.

Gabriel watched Bev and Mo dart furtive glances at each other when they thought there was no chance of being caught. Mo looked at his daughter with quiet longing written in her eyes. Bev stared back at this woman turned child with a trace of bewilderment and confusion. It was difficult not to like someone as spontaneous as Mo, but Bev was trying as hard as she could. The fact that Mo seemed not to notice that she was being ignored was perplexing to Bev, he could see. And he thanked Mo from the bottom of his heart for not giving up. Breaking through Bev's walls wasn't easy, and yet she kept trying.

As lunchtime gave way to afternoon, Mo turned to Bev. "What's next on the agenda? You know this place best."

Gabriel glanced at his watch. They'd already gotten splashed, whipped about in circles, turned upside down and plummeted through empty space. After a hot dog with fries, Mo was beginning to look a bit pale.

"Why don't we just sit for a while," he suggested. "Take a short rest."

"All right," Bev agreed, climbing up on a stool near a table. But it was obvious by her squirming little body that she would rather do anything but rest.

Mo was studying his daughter too, Gabriel saw. "You sure?" she asked. "I'm not really tired. Are you, Bev? We could do something else while your dad rests for a few minutes."

Bev's eyes lit up with sudden delight. "Yeah, we could ride the Spiro-coaster. It's the biggest one in the park, and Dad hates it."

Gabriel could almost see Mo's pallor deepen an entire shade. "I don't think so, Bev," he said. "That's a bit much after all that food, don't you think? You might get sick."

"Daddy, you know I never get sick. Not like you. It would be all right, wouldn't it? You wouldn't mind if it was just Mo and me, would you?"

Mo was pale, but her eyes said "please" just as clearly as Bev's voice did.

"Of course I wouldn't mind if you went alone with Mo, but I don't—" he began.

And then Mo actually said it. "Please." Her soft voice hit him square in the gut.

PLAY

BIG BUCKS

ONE MILLION

ONE MILLION

AND YOU COULD WIN THE

$1,000,000,000.00

PLUS JACKPOT!

SILHOUETTE

YOUR PERSONAL
GAME CARD
INSIDE...

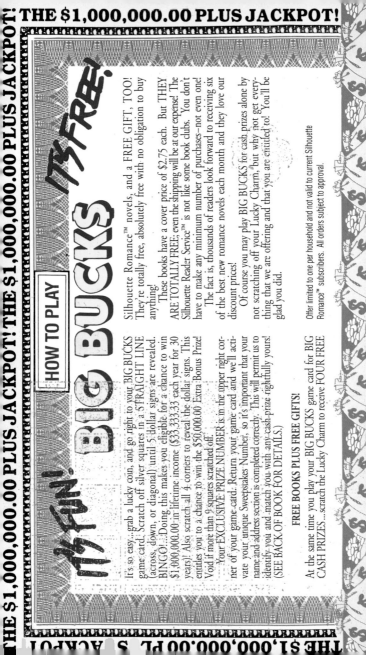

IT'S FUN! BIG BUCKS IT'S FREE!

HOW TO PLAY

It's so easy...grab a lucky coin, and go right to your BIG BUCKS game card. Scratch off silver squares in a STRAIGHT LINE (across, down, or diagonal) until 5 dollar signs are revealed. BINGO!...Doing this makes you eligible for a chance to win $1,000,000.00 in lifetime income ($33,333.33 each year for 30 years)! Also scratch all 4 corners to reveal the dollar signs. This entitles you to a chance to win the $50,000.00 Extra Bonus Prize! Void if more than 9 squares scratched off.

Your EXCLUSIVE PRIZE NUMBER is in the upper right corner of your game card. Return your game card and we'll activate your unique Sweepstakes Number, so it's important that your name and address section is completed correctly. This will permit us to identify you and match you with any cash prize rightfully yours! (SEE BACK OF BOOK FOR DETAILS.)

FREE BOOKS PLUS FREE GIFTS!

At the same time you play your BIG BUCKS game card for BIG CASH PRIZES...scratch the Lucky Charm to receive FOUR FREE

Silhouette Romance™ novels, and a FREE GIFT, TOO! They're totally free, absolutely free with no obligation to buy anything!

These books have a cover price of $2.75 each. But THEY ARE TOTALLY FREE; even the shipping will be at our expense! The Silhouette Reader Service™ is not like some book clubs. You don't have to make any minimum number of purchases—not even one!

The fact is, thousands of readers look forward to receiving six of the best new romance novels each month and they love our discount prices!

Of course you may play BIG BUCKS for cash prizes alone by not scratching off your Lucky Charm, but why not get everything that we are offering and that you are entitled to! You'll be glad you did.

Offer limited to one per household and not valid to current Silhouette Romance™ subscribers. All orders subject to approval.

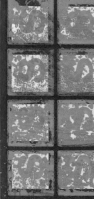

THE SILHOUETTE READER SERVICE™: HERE'S HOW IT WORKS

Accepting free books places you under no obligation to buy anything. You may keep the books and gift and return the shipping statement marked "cancel". If you do not cancel, about a month later we will send you 6 additional novels and bill you just $2.19 each plus 25¢ delivery and applicable sales tax, if any.* That's the complete price, and – compared to cover prices of $2.75 each – quite a bargain! You may cancel at any time, but if you choose to continue, every month we'll send you 6 more books, which you may either purchase at the discount price...or return at our expense and cancel your subscription.

*Terms and prices subject to change without notice. Sales tax applicable in N.Y.

He was used to his daughter's demands, he knew how to deal with her childish pleadings. Most of the time. But this was a grown woman. A woman who fascinated him. A woman who was asking him for something that only he could give. Looking into her eyes, Gabe could see that Mo realized how extraordinary Bev's small request to do something without him was.

"All right. Once," he agreed. "But only once. Then you both come right back here and sit down."

Nodding solemnly like children, when only one of them, in fact, was a child, Mo and Bev wandered away, not really speaking, but not avoiding each other, either.

Mo stood in the line, waiting with Bev. She didn't try to fool herself into believing that the little girl was here with her out of any real need to share her company. Like most children, she had simply seen an opportunity to do what she wanted . . . and she had taken it. Mo was a means to an end, a chance to ride on the roller coaster that Bev knew her father disliked.

Don't do this, Mo's stomach warned, giving a lurch.

Looking down at Bev, she ignored it. It was only her imagination and a few memories she'd been planning to discard, anyway. Nothing more. She was not a little girl anymore. She could control her mind and her body's responses. She tried not to think about the number of times Gabriel's nearness had proved her wrong.

"Have you been on this before?" she asked Bev.

"Once," the girl replied absently. "I nearly threw up, but it was worth it." When she looked up at Mo, her eyes were dancing, alight with the kind of excitement that only children knew.

Mo hazarded a smile back.

Bev quickly looked down at her toes.

"Does your mother like amusement parks?" Mo asked. No point in acting like the woman didn't exist, she decided.

"Not really," Bev said, shaking her head. "When I was little, we all went together, and she always took me on the merry-go-round. But now I'm too big for that. It's definitely for babies. And Harry doesn't like stuff like this where people scream so much."

Harry was sounding more and more like a wet rag, Mo thought. But she also knew that Bev didn't think very highly of her, either, so she didn't want to judge. Besides, it wouldn't be wise to say anything negative about a man who might easily end up being Bev's stepfather.

"Maybe Harry has sensitive eardrums," she offered lamely.

Bev merely looked up and frowned.

They were at the front of the line now, and Mo could feel her heart and her stomach beginning to pulse. Carefully, she swallowed back her trepidation and stepped forward, climbing into the seat. Too late to change her mind now. She was fine. She was *not* going to give in to some childish memory of humiliation in front of a crowd. Everything would be fine.

Those were the words that she kept repeating to herself from those first exhilarating moments of free fall to the very second when her stomach began to churn furiously. Swallowing hard, Mo struggled simply to hang on, to keep her eyes open so that she couldn't give in to the sickening dizziness, to keep breathing air. In and out. In and out.

Beside her, Bev was squealing in sheer delight, and Mo wished that she could conjure up a grin so she could turn to the little girl and share in her joy.

But Mother Nature would have none of it. All Mo could do was hang on and hope that the end would come soon.

When it did, she drew in deep drafts of air, holding herself immobile for long seconds before following Bev down the steps to the solid feel of ground beneath her feet.

Mo knew that her face must be positively green; she was struggling hard to keep her lunch down.

And Gabriel was standing before her, a concerned look creasing his brow. "I can't believe I was foolish enough to have let you go. Come on, let's get you to a seat."

Mo closed her eyes finally, grateful for the warm, comforting feel of Gabriel's big hand on the small of her back. Sitting down, she felt the nausea begin to fade, just a bit.

She slid a sideways glance at Bev, wondering if she had totally flunked the kid test. "I thought things might have changed," she confided. "Looks like I still get sick on roller coasters. My father always told me that it was all in my head, but he was wrong. It's definitely in my stomach."

Her small attempt at a joke was met with silence.

Bev was staring at her with dark, round eyes. "You knew you'd get sick and you still went on?"

Mo started to shake her head, then realized the folly of doing something so insane. "Grown-ups," she managed. "You just can't figure them, can you? Sometimes they do the stupidest things."

Bev bit her lip and didn't say a word.

A few minutes later, when the worst of her seasick feeling had passed, Gabriel surged to his feet. "Come on," he said, holding out a hand to Mo. "We'd better get you home."

Mo knew darn well that it was only two in the afternoon and that Bev had been counting on a full day of fun. "No, I'm fine here. You guys go see some more things. I'm just going to sit here a few more minutes." At Gabriel's protest, Mo shook her head vehemently. "Are you going to argue with a sick woman, Gabriel? I assure you that if you get me too upset right now, there could be dire consequences. I could erupt like Mount Vesuvius any minute," she explained more explicitly. "Go. Please. I'll be fine."

Gabriel opened his mouth once again, and she shook her head. Too hard. "Believe me, you wouldn't want to put me in a moving vehicle right now. Any vehicle. Including a car. Bev," she ordered, "go on and take your dad off somewhere. I'm really okay. Just a little embarrassed. It's not every day I change colors in front of other human beings."

Bev nodded solemnly and even added a tiny smile. "We could have ridden the merry-go-round," she said, just before she went. "Next time we will."

They were the simplest, sweetest words Mo had ever heard.

Only an hour later, they were back home. Gabriel and Bev had returned in ten minutes, with Gabriel insisting that they take Mo home. While Bev hadn't really said anything, she hadn't looked upset about the unexpected end to the day.

Mo slept during the ride home and awoke to see Bev disappearing into the house to call some friends. Wandering into the kitchen herself, she prepared to make plans for dinner.

She took a battered cookbook off the top shelf next to the refrigerator and turned to see Gabriel standing there.

"What are you doing now?" he asked, reaching for the book.

She looked down to where the book had fallen open in her palms. Shrugging, she raised her brows. "Learning to prepare quesadillas? I guess I'm just feeling a little south of the border tonight."

"More like a little under the weather, I'd say. I shouldn't have let you stay as long as I did."

Mo carefully laid the book on a counter, then crossed her arms in front of her. "I'm not a little girl, Gabriel. You don't have to protect me and handle me with such care."

He reached out, brushing a stray tendril from her forehead, then pushed the book farther aside. When he looked at her, his eyes were dark and bold. "I know you're not a little girl, Mo. Don't think I ever thought differently. You're a woman, a fully grown, exquisitely made woman, and I'm very aware of that. Always."

He was a breath away. She could have reached out and touched him, pushed into his arms, wrapped herself about the hard, male beauty of him. The urge to do so was sweet, compelling torture. But the fear of how it would end was far too frightening to let her put her wishes into motion. She knew all too well that she was capable of confusing one thing for another. He was a man who desired her, who perhaps was grateful for her interest in his daughter, but it would go no farther than that. She would have to remember that, to be careful and keep watch over her feelings.

Mo stared up at Gabriel, feeling herself go paler, swaying on matchstick legs.

With arms of steel he gathered her close and pulled her to a chair. Gently he lowered her, kneeling beside her with a small curse.

"You've had quite a day—loops, spins, drops, twirls. You did it all, didn't you?"

Mo looked up, smiling shakily. "Oh, come on, it was fun. Admit it, you enjoyed yourself, too. Until I did my amazing rainbow act."

The look on Gabriel's face could only be called sheepish. "All right, I felt a little dumb having my knees touch my nose on some of the smaller stuff, but I admit it, I had fun. You were good to Bev."

"She was good about going home. I just wish I could have managed the roller coaster. I never could. My father hated that, the fact that I always got sick on the rough stuff."

He lifted a lock of her hair, rubbing it between his fingers. "You weren't close to your father, were you?"

Mo shook her head, locking her fingers together into a painted grip. "No, but believe me, I wasn't alone on his blacklist. My father cursed my mother eternally for leaving him with five kids when he hadn't wanted children in the first place. Especially me. I think he blamed me for the fact that my brothers didn't have the least interest in sports. Artistic sorts, every one, and all due to my careless female influence. Or that's how he reasoned it out. I was a major disappointment to him. But...I had Aunt Rose, thank goodness. She saved me from getting too maudlin many, many times."

Mo peeked up at Gabriel's suddenly sad eyes and ran her fingers down between his bunched brows. "Don't waste your time feeling sorry for me, Gabriel. It was all a long, long time ago. As you pointed out, I'm a full-grown woman now and master of my own fate. I've got my own life, my own career, my own goals. I'm a woman of the world."

"And a good sport," he added on a grin. "Did anyone ever tell you that?"

Turning in her seat, Mo leaned back in her chair, doing her best to look down her nose. "Yes, as a matter of fact. Billy Wilkins once told me that very thing—in fourth grade, when I passed him the answers to the math test."

Gabriel leaned over Mo, covering one of her hands with his own. "I guess Billy Wilkins knew a smart lady when he saw one."

"Yes, well, don't give him too much praise," Mo said with a sniff. "He also called me ugly, skinny, and barked like a dog whenever he saw me."

"Obviously a real lady-killer," Gabe noted.

"Obviously," Mo agreed.

"So..." Gabriel slid his hand up her bare arm to her shoulder. "Does that mean he never did this?" he asked, inching closer and slipping both arms about her. "Or this?"

His words ended on a whisper as he lowered his lips and touched her mouth in one quick, gentle pass.

A soft groan escaped Gabriel's lips. Mo thought her heart would break if she didn't kiss him back.

She managed to keep her arms at her side as she turned her face away and swallowed. "Of course not," she choked out. "I would have socked him."

He laced his fingers through her hair, turning her to him once more, holding her face still so that she was staring into his eyes. "I suppose I should apologize," he said. "I seem to remember telling you once that I wouldn't do that anymore."

"Oh, you don't have to worry," she whispered, nervously licking her lips. "I don't think I have the energy to punch you in the nose right now."

Immediately Gabriel's eyes grew dark with concern. "You did too much today. And I was a jerk for letting you stay at the park. I should have gotten you home a long time ago." And without another word, he scooped her up into his arms.

"What are you doing?" she whispered. "I have to make dinner."

"I'm taking you upstairs to tuck you into bed," he answered, ignoring her halfhearted protests. "The only thing you're going to be doing tonight is dreaming."

"I could walk," Mo insisted, squirming against his chest.

"You could fall down on your feet, too. If there's one thing I've learned about you today, Mo, it's that you don't know when to quit. So I'm not giving you the chance to run yourself into the ground anymore today. I'm not your father, Mo. You don't have to prove to me that you can run with the pack."

"But I can," she said stubbornly.

"I know." He stopped at the top of the stairs and looked into her eyes. "I know you can. You just don't have to prove it to me. You don't have to prove anything to me. All right?"

She wanted to tell him that she didn't work too hard to please people anymore. But Gabriel was walking again, and she was too tired to force the words out. She didn't trust herself not to say something stupid. Her voice wouldn't work.

But her *eyes* worked just fine when she looked back down the hall and saw the little face peeping out at her from the doorway behind Gabriel's shoulder. Bev stood in her nightdress, on one little naked foot, the other tucked under her like a fragile flamingo. Her eyes stared back at Mo, big and round and scared...and accusing.

Then the little girl was gone, the door swinging shut with a tiny bump. Mo was left wondering how she had ever had the audacity to blithely announce to the world that she was the perfect candidate for motherhood. How could she ever say that again with those sad, lonely eyes following her into her dreams?

Chapter Six

Mo was staring into her empty coffee cup the next morning when Gabriel came into the kitchen.

"Something interesting in there?"

Startled, Mo rose to her feet, wondering how Gabriel managed to look so alert this early in the morning. She felt like she had just crawled out of the blankets. Moreover, she was sure that her face still bore the imprints of her wrinkled sheets as evidence of her restless dreams.

Needing to keep busy, to stop thinking about how the evening had ended, she rose and pulled another mug from the cupboard. Automatically she picked up the half-full pot and carried it to the table.

"Sit down, Mo. Please. Today we're going to 'do the zoo' as Bev says. But that's after we go out for breakfast. So there's no need for you to keep hopping up and down."

Nodding, she sat, refilled her cup and reached to pick it up.

He caught her hand in his own. "If you're rested, you're coming with us, right?"

Mo stared at his flesh against hers. It was amazing, alarming how the slightest touch from this man could draw a response from her. It was also foolish . . . and forbidden, she thought, remembering her own promises to herself, remembering Bev's eyes the night before.

"No. No, you go without me. I have a little headache." At his raised eyebrows, she frowned. "Really, I do," she insisted.

Gabriel lifted her chin with one finger, forcing her to stare into his eyes. It wasn't fair that he should be able to affect her so easily. She couldn't bear the look of concern in his eyes. She couldn't deal with the fear that he might kiss her again. Or that she wanted him to when she knew that she shouldn't.

"If you aren't well, you should be in bed," he admonished, smoothing her brow with the tips of his fingers, pulling her to her feet.

"It's not anything serious," she said, knowing that her voice was hesitant and defensive. "I'll be fine soon." Her hands were trembling in his own.

Gabriel frowned in disbelief. "Why don't you go lie down for a while? We don't have to leave now," he suggested, watching as Mo quickly removed her hands from his grasp and tucked them into her back pockets. "Bev isn't even up yet. She won't care if we get started a little late. She won't mind waiting for you."

He was wrong. Mo knew that, but she didn't want to say so. He hadn't seen his daughter's stricken face the night before. Mo didn't want him to know or to worry. It was up to her to defuse the situation and keep her distance. As she hesitated, searching for the right words, the phone rang in the hallway.

And Gabriel was proven wrong in more ways than one.

Bev wasn't asleep. She came tripping down the stairs, diving for the phone seconds before Gabriel or Mo could reach it. Her pint-size gym shoes dangled by their hot pink strings, held tightly in one hand as she pushed the receiver underneath her dark curls in search of an ear.

The voice on the other end of the line was loud, loud enough for Mo to hear it inside the kitchen doorway.

Bev held the receiver away from her, frowning, just before she laid it on the table.

"It's for you, Dad," she said, sitting on the floor to put her sneakers on. "That Smithson guy."

Smithson, Mo knew, was Gabriel's next-in-charge at the office.

Gabriel took the call in his office.

Fifteen minutes later, he emerged, studying Bev beneath bunched brows.

"I have to go in to work for a while," he confessed. "It's an emergency, cupcake."

Bev stared at him, playing with a strand of her hair. "Can I come with you?"

Mo pretended to be busy cleaning the mirror in the hallway.

"Not this time. Another day," he promised, ruffling her curls. "Right now, there's glass all over the place. One of the employees managed to run a car through the window of the building right into the lobby, and everyone's a little nutty right now. I take it that the media is crawling all over the place, and Smithson's drinking antacid like it was water."

At Gabriel's critical use of the word *media,* Mo raised her hands in self-defense. "I only write fiction these days, and I've only been up fifteen minutes," she explained. "Is everyone all right?"

"I think so," he said, nodding. "Fortunately the office hadn't been open long, so there weren't many people there yet. But a few employees did get shaken up and are being kept at the hospital for observation. Smithson's having trouble covering all the bases without me there. But I'll try to be back early," he promised. "Can you manage?"

Mo exchanged a look with Bev. The girl's eyes were wary, refusing to hold still for Mo to study her expression.

"We'll manage," Mo promised. She knew her voice sounded less than firm, but Gabriel gave a grateful smile and nodded, his dark blue gaze settling on her, letting her know that he trusted her.

A few minutes later, his tie still dangling, he grabbed his briefcase and disappeared through the door.

Silence spread through the kitchen like a disease.

"So," Mo began, putting down her cloth, "should we go to the zoo?"

Bev bit her lip, looking Mo over. "Do you want to?"

Opening her mouth to agree, Mo suddenly stopped. She folded her arms, watching Bev's eyes. "Do you like going to the zoo?"

Bev's blue eyes narrowed just before she turned away with another shrug. "Dad likes to take me," she confessed.

"That's not what I asked you."

"We don't have to go," Bev admitted, and Mo knew as surely as she knew anything that the appeal of the zoo had simply been the company, not the thrill of seeing the lions and tigers.

"We could do something else."

The little girl-woman turned to Mo. "Why?"

"Why what?"

Bev lifted her head suddenly and stared Mo full in the face. "Why would you want to take me somewhere when I've been mean to you? I made you so sick yesterday that Dad even had to carry you up the stairs. Aren't you mad about that? I figured you would be."

Mo pushed a hand through the length of her curls, mussing them. This was something she hadn't expected. It confused her to find out that what she'd seen in Bev's eyes last night hadn't been hurt, but fear, possibly even remorse. It seemed they were both feeling guilty...for all the wrong reasons.

Suddenly Mo smiled and sat down on the floor next to the child. "I'm the one who climbed on the roller coaster, Bev. You didn't drag me."

An ordinary ten-year-old might have accepted that, but hadn't Gabriel warned her that Bev was more adult than child? "Mom says sometimes I wheedle her into getting my way when I want something badly enough."

Mo did allow herself a laugh at that. "One of the most unfortunate things about being an adult is that you can't blame anyone but yourself for the things you do. I knew that I was going to crawl off that roller coaster with a bad case of the spins, but I went, anyway. Because *I* wanted to, not because you 'wheedled' me into it. Now, what do you say— are we going to go somewhere today or not? There's still a whole day ahead of us."

Bev nodded slightly and ventured a tiny smile. "What else can we do if we skip the zoo? Dad really likes the animals. I'd rather not go without him." Her voice trailed off wistfully and it was clear that, for all her grown-up ways, Bev was just a little girl who'd been cheated out of a day of her father's precious company.

Mo contemplated her decision. She could have named a thousand different things designed to appeal to a near adolescent, some more exciting than others, but there was only one she could think of that would have any attraction for Bev right now.

"We—we could go visit your dad at his office."

Bev tilted her head to the side. Her dark blue eyes narrowed slightly, but there was hope written on her face. Her time with Gabriel was slipping away like sand through splayed fingers. "Dad said I couldn't come with him."

"I meant after they've cleaned up, when he has a few minutes of free time. While we're waiting we can go get our nails done. Blue with lots of glitter, I think," Mo said, holding her naked fingernails for Bev's inspection.

To her surprise, Bev's face glowed with new interest, and a devilish light appeared in her eyes. "Purple with flowers," she corrected, examining her own pale fingernails.

"Okay, blue and purple with glitter *and* flowers. Let me just change my blouse."

"Yeah," Bev agreed as Mo rose and turned away. "Mo?" she called.

Mo stopped, her body still twisting into the turn. She waited for Bev to speak.

"Thanks. But don't tell my mom," Bev said, ducking her head. "She thinks it's really gross to decorate your nails."

Wonderful. Now she'd done it, Mo thought, wondering if she should try to wiggle free of the commitment she'd just made. But Bev was beaming at her, and Mo remembered the small forbidden pleasures Aunt Rose had gifted her with in the past, the things that had made her loneliness fade away into the distance. What the heck, it was only polish and glitter and could be removed at the end of the day. But Bev would have fun. Gaudy fingernails and a forbidden trip to her father's office. Folding her arms with sudden determination, Mo grinned.

"Race you to the top of the stairs," she said with a wink. "Winner gets her nails done first."

Bev's eyes lit up and she sprinted toward the landing, easily besting Mo.

"I win," she declared with a laugh.

No, I do, Mo thought. Bev had let down her fences, just a touch.

It was funny how things could get out of hand, Mo thought, staring at the bright lights of the Bonner Hardware corporate offices. A simple trip to jazz up two sets of nails had turned into a full-fledged, go-crazy shopping bender complete with a side tour of one of the Bonner Hardware stores. Mo smiled, remembering how serious Bev had been as she studied the bins of black, cast-iron "elbows," pondered all the possible uses for an "adjustable spud," and shyly mentioned that she loved the smell of lumber. With a little coaxing, she had even offered to help Mo pick out a book on home repair for her ever-expanding library. It had been a small beginning.

Now, after a full day of store-hopping, Bev was wearing a big, blue floppy hat she hadn't owned that morning, and Mo had a pair of rhinestone sunglasses perched on her head that she would have passed up on any other day. The glasses were silly things, even for Mo, but Bev had admired them tremendously, and it had been far too hard to resist her soft-spoken enthusiasm.

The whirlwind shopping trip had been a success, but by now the day was well advanced. The initial roar of the morning's trauma at Bonner's had died down to a high-tension hum. Mo looked up Gabriel's name on the directory on the wall.

"We should stop at the front desk and send a message that you're here," Mo suggested.

Bev shook her head, causing the hat to slip down over her eyes. "No," she said, pushing it back. "I want to surprise him. I want him to see how I look."

Taking in a deep breath, Mo considered that option. She glanced at Bev, wondering if Gabriel would think she'd been too impulsive in indulging his daughter. They had come here against his express wishes. The little girl was wearing a hat that was two sizes too big, her nails glowed like neon on black velvet, her hair was a wild tangle slipping out from beneath the hideous hat. There was a smudge on her cheek from where she'd brushed against the car in the parking lot. She was bedraggled. She was smiling.

Nodding, Mo gave in and silently agreed to suffer the consequences of Gabriel's disapproval if need be. Every little girl should have a few days of unfettered freedom, even if there was a price to pay later.

They rode up to the top floor on an elevator that made any of the rooms in Mo's tiny apartment look sadly deficient. The scent of citrus pervaded the plush compartment, and Mo was reminded of what totally different circles she and Gabriel traveled in.

Mo looked down at Bev and somehow continued to look confident, but when they stepped out of the elevator into the elegant surroundings of the Bonner Hardware nerve center, it was Bev who was clearly leading the way.

She tripped down the hallway without missing a step, walking up to the receptionist with the regal bearing of a born leader.

Ignoring her wilted appearance, she raised her little chin in the air. "I'm here to see my father," she declared. "And I'd rather not be announced, if that's all right. Is he around, do you think?"

The woman didn't even bother asking who "he" was. She tilted her head in an elegant acknowledgment of Bev, smiled apologetically at Mo and motioned toward a door behind her.

"He *was* hiding in there a short while ago," she admitted. "It's been quite a busy day. But I'm afraid you've missed him. He's already gone home."

Bev's sophisticated act melted like ice cream on a steaming sidewalk. She sucked in her lower lip and her shoulders sank a quarter of an inch.

"Come on," Mo encouraged, forgetting herself enough to throw a careless arm around those sad little shoulders. "My old clunker will get us home in no time."

For a minute, Mo could almost see Gabriel's face in the disbelieving rise of Bev's eyebrows. "*Your* car?" she squeaked.

"Hey, it's old, but it's dependable," Mo insisted.

Two hours later, the tow-truck driver dropped the car in the drive, took the entire remaining contents of Mo's wallet and drove away. At least, Mo thought, Bev had taken the whole episode in stride. She'd been excited at the prospect of doing something so foreign to her upbringing as riding in the cab of a tow truck. Not once had she said, "I told you so."

Dragging into the house, carrying a sweating bag of egg foo yong she had insisted the driver stop for, Mo was met by Gabriel's blue-eyed devilish smile.

Propped against the hallway credenza with his arms crossed, he looked as cool as an April evening. As for Mo, frustration and heat had wilted her hair, her rhinestone sunglasses had slid down her nose, and her newly painted nails felt as though they were melting away to drip down onto the floor.

But Gabriel was smiling at her over the top of his daughter's head. And Mo realized that Bev had launched into an animated account of her day, her delicate hands swaying, the floppy hat dipping as she recounted every exciting moment, from the sequined flowers on her fingertips to the surprise ride home with Jeff of Jeff and Al's Towing.

"Do you like my hat?" Bev said, suddenly stopping and leaning over so he could see the button trim on the top.

"I love it," he assured her.

Mo felt her eyes grow wide at that. The hat didn't look like something Gabriel would have chosen, but she caught his grin over the top of Bev's head and couldn't help smiling back.

"I love it," he repeated. "Did you pick it out yourself, cupcake?"

"Of course," Bev said indignantly. "Daddy, I'm not so little that I can't choose my own things. I picked out Mo's glasses, too."

"I thought so," he said hesitantly, raising those brows again. "Well, they're certainly..."

"Glittery," Mo provided, rushing in as she pushed the huge frames back up on her nose.

"Thank you. Just the word I was looking for. You look glittery. Shining. Both of you." And Mo knew that it wasn't the rhinestones he was referring to. Bev was still glowing, basking in her father's praise. They were *all* glowing.

"Daddy, we came to see you, but you were already gone home," Bev admonished solemnly. "I was going to surprise you."

"I know," Gabriel said, bending down on one knee before her. "My secretary called me after you left. And I'm sorry, but it was nice to be here when you got home. Now go on up to your room and get ready for dinner. It's getting late."

When she had gathered her packages, Bev skipped to the stairs. Mo looked down at the wilting food bag in her arms.

"Sorry about dinner. I figured you'd rather eat take-out than wait till I could get something on. We were later than I'd planned."

"It doesn't matter, Mo. Besides, something has come up. Cynthia called while you were gone."

"Cynthia?" Mo remembered the last time her sister-in-law had called. That was when she'd kept Winnie and brought that sad look to Gabriel's face.

"Don't look so stricken," Gabriel soothed, moving toward her. "She just needs a baby-sitter again."

Immediately Mo moved to the phone. "I'll call her right back and tell her that I can't," she promised softly.

"And make a liar out of me?" he asked, touching her hand where she held the receiver. Gently he took the phone from her and placed it back in its cradle. "When I already told her yes?"

"You told her yes?" she asked disbelievingly, feeling her heart start to kick up at his nearness.

"You don't want to baby-sit? I thought you loved babies," he admonished.

"I do, but—"

"You're not going to desert me now, are you?" he asked. "If you don't help me, I'll have to do it all alone. And I'm not quite sure I've got what it takes." He rubbed his fingers across his brow as if he was genuinely worried.

Mo remembered the day that Winnie had been here, the total wreck the house had been, and suddenly she smiled in sympathy.

"Oh, come on," she teased. "After all, Winnie's only one little baby." One very active baby, she amended to herself, still not sure why Gabriel had told Cynthia she'd baby-sit when he'd objected so strongly before.

"Umm... not quite," Gabriel said. A slow pink flush suffused his face.

"Not quite what?"

"Not quite just one little baby."

At Mo's confused expression, he ran a hand through his hair, ruffling it, then making things worse by passing his other hand through it. He loosened his tie, a sure sign that something was amiss.

Mo stood waiting, one corner of her mouth twisted up.

"Cynthia got called away unexpectedly," he explained. "And she was baby-sitting, herself. For your cousin Amy, it seems."

Mo slid her hands up over her mouth, trying to hold the laughter back.

"And Amy..." Gabriel gave up, looking to Mo for help.

"Has five children," Mo supplied, helpless to stop her grin from showing.

"Well, yes, but the oldest is at a sleepover," Gabriel assured her.

"That's reassuring," she acknowledged, widening her eyes. "Gabriel, why did you ever agree to this crazy scheme when I know it goes against everything you're feeling?"

Leaning back against the wall, he blew out a puff of air and crossed his arms over his chest. "It doesn't," he said. "When Bev is here, I just want her to be happy. And to have kids in the house, a baby…. She'll adore that. Besides," he admitted, lowering his voice, "you'll love it, too. I know you will. And, after all, it's just a small gathering."

"Gabriel," Mo said slowly. "Five children and one small adult is hardly a small gathering. It's an event, a group, a party. There are small towns with fewer people than that."

He leaned closer then, his arms still crossed, but his face only inches from her own. "A small town, huh? You aren't going to desert me, are you?"

She licked her lips, wishing she didn't feel so unsettled whenever he was near. "I wouldn't desert you," she said softly.

"I'll remember that," he said.

And Mo wondered what exactly she had agreed to.

Chapter Seven

Sometime during the next several hours, Mo looked across the top of Bev's head at Gabriel. Bev sat next to Mo holding Winnie. Ben and Mike, aged nine and eight, were in the other room watching television. For the last hour or two Gabriel had played board games, supervised races in the backyard and helped Mo dish out kid food. Now he had the twins, Josh and Sam, two rough-and-tumble four-year-olds, on either knee, and he was telling them a story about knights and dragons and little blue creatures that lived beneath the earth.

They were fascinated. *Mo* was fascinated, enthralled, enchanted.

"And then what happened?" Josh asked, raking his chubby fist across the lapel of Gabriel's charcoal-gray designer suit.

Gabriel seemed not to notice, but Mo did. His suit was wrinkled, his tie was loose and crushed. His white shirt had stains where small fingers had picked at the buttons.

Mo looked around at Gabriel's magnificent house. She couldn't hold back her soft gasp.

Gabriel raised his head from his story. His eyes met hers across the room.

"It's only a house, Mo," he told her.

How did he do that? she wondered. How did he manage to be so sophisticated and so artfully laid-back at the same time?

And it wasn't "only a house." This house hadn't been decorated with children in mind. Mo knew that. There would never be any children other than Bev. And yet, for a short time, Gabriel had ignored the fact that someone had spilled juice on his coffee table, that his clothes would probably have to be burned. He was sitting there weaving a story, and the two little boys, with their round, long-lashed eyes and their juice-covered mouths open circles of wonder, were absolutely spellbound. This from a man who would never have another child in his life.

Mo wondered at the kinds of demons he'd wrestled with before coming to that decision, and she was ashamed at her own too easy demands for a child.

Her eyes misted over, and she caught Gabriel's quick look of concern. He stumbled over the next part of the story, then paused.

"I'll help you clean it up," he offered.

Mo blinked back the dampness. She noticed the way Gabriel's arm was supporting a wobbly Josh from falling from his perch, the way he didn't seem to mind that there was a smudge of chocolate on the leg of his pants. And she was almost sure that if she didn't get out of here right now, she was not going to be able to keep one or two tears from slipping down. If she didn't leave right now, this very minute, she was going to march right over there and throw herself into Gabriel's arms.

But of course she couldn't leave. And she couldn't fling herself at Gabriel, either.

"Thank you," she finally managed with a prim little nod.

She shifted in her seat, and finally noticed that Bev had fallen asleep. The little girl had slipped over, her cheek pressed up against Mo's side, her hair tangled. Gently Mo lifted the baby off Bev's lap, cuddling Winnie against her other side. Gabriel's child, the daughter of his dreams, sighed and wrapped her arms about Mo in a gesture of trust. She squirmed and positioned herself more comfortably, her breath warm against Mo's body. In her sleep, Bev smiled.

And Mo's tears really did begin to fall then.

Looking up at Gabriel, she saw that he was smiling at her, that his eyes were dark and glowing and fierce.

Josh, young and oblivious to the wonder of Bev's actions, pulled on Gabriel's sleeve, demanding that he get back to the story, that he save the princess from the tower before the dragon had time to get close enough to eat her.

Gabriel looked down and began to speak, his smile growing as he told a preposterous tale of how the princess saved herself and gained her freedom by winning the dragon over to her side with love and patience and bits of Oreo crumbs.

Josh and Daniel oohed and aahed at that one, and begged for another story.

But Mo smiled slowly to herself, pulled Winnie more closely to her and stroked Bev's hair as the little girl slept on.

She could feel Gabriel's eyes resting on her, and she knew without a doubt that leaving this man was going to be much, much harder than she had ever imagined. She knew that taking this job had been both the smartest thing she'd ever done and, undeniably, the most foolish. She had fought against every feeling that had been growing for Gabriel since the day she'd walked into his house . . . and she had lost.

The only thing to do now was to brace herself for the inevitable ending.

Watching her with his daughter, Gabriel could barely swallow. Bev was snuggled up against Mo as if she'd been sleeping that way all her life.

Mo was stroking Bev's hair as if she were the most precious child ever to grace the earth.

When the doorbell rang, Mo started to rise, but Gabe stopped her with a look. "Just stay right there," he said. "I'll get the kids ready to go."

A grateful smile was his reward. Which he cherished.

While Mo's cousin, Amy, pried the older boys loose from the television, Gabriel struggled to fit Winnie into a too snug hooded sweater. When he was done, the buttons weren't quite straight, but she was covered.

"Good girl," he coaxed when she raised her soft little chin to let him tie the strings on her hood.

Winnie sparkled and cooed her delight at his praise. She made smacking noises with her baby rosebud lips, and Gabriel leaned forward, accepting the wet kiss on his cheek.

Josh and Sam flapped and turned, twisting until they found the sleeves of their own lightweight jackets, then patiently waiting for Gabe to help them with the bothersome zippers.

"I liked that story," Sam said as Gabe inched the zipper past the wad of Sam's shirt that was sticking out. "You got more?"

Gabriel looked across to where Mo sat, suddenly wary and watchful. Her hand had stilled on Bev's curls.

"Some," Gabe admitted. "You like hearing stories?"

Sam's nod was solemn and slow. He nudged Josh in the ribs with his elbow. Josh nodded, too.

"Mommy works. She's tired lots," Josh volunteered. "Ain't got no daddy to tell us stories like you did. We could come, me and Sam, maybe. Sometimes."

Mo was shaking her head. "Josh," she began gently, but Gabriel turned and shook his head back at her, trying to let her know that it was okay.

"Bev will be here for a few more days," he said. "Come soon."

"And you'll tell us stories? You know more?"

"I'll think of some, Sam," he promised. "I'll try to think of something good between now and then."

Gabriel boosted Winnie into his arms and motioned Josh and Sam to follow him to where their mother was waiting at the door. Amy was a tired, wan woman whose face bore the strain of too many responsibilities at too young an age.

She took Winnie from Gabe and dropped a kiss on Sam's and Josh's forehead.

"Thank you," she said. "I don't like to ask for help, but sometimes—"

Gabe placed his hand on her arm. "They were a joy," he assured her.

Her smile told him something he would never have guessed otherwise. She had once been young and lovely, not so long ago.

But worry still lurked in the corners of her eyes as she turned to him, the door half-open.

"Mo's a very good person," she said slowly. "And she's not always had the kind of life she should. Be careful of her."

It was a warning as clear as water in a crystal vase, but no clearer than the ones he'd been issuing to himself for weeks, Gabe knew. Closing the door, he moved to the window, looking out into the blackness.

He watched until the woman had driven away...and then he watched some more, thinking.

Mo.

From the moment he'd met her, she'd filled him with dark desire he'd tried to ignore. But tonight, seeing her close to Bev, he'd felt things . . . longings—strong and urgent. And the warning bells in his head had been clanging hard ever since.

This was a woman who was, as her cousin had said, a good person. This was a woman he longed for with an intensity that was frightening and fierce. She'd said she didn't want a husband, and he had to believe her. She was determined and bold and independent.

Yet when he looked into her eyes, when she was close against him, in his arms, her heart fluttered like a small, helpless animal caught in a trap. She was a woman who could be hurt so easily, if the man wasn't careful, if he made the wrong move or wasn't sure. And *he* wasn't.

He wasn't sure. Not at all. He was scared—damn scared—of what he felt when he looked at her, when he touched her, when she spoke or moved or simply walked into a room. He could barely control himself. And control had always been the key to happiness as far as he was concerned. Letting go led to pain, and tragedy. If he gave in without knowing his own mind, without studying the consequences, without being totally, absolutely sure, he knew he would hurt her. And he'd never be able to live with himself after that.

Kicking around in this big old house, knowing he'd dimmed the brightness of her soul, he'd be lost once and for all. He'd be no good for anyone. Not for Mo, not for himself, not for Bev. And he had to be there, one hundred per cent, for Bev.

"Gabriel?" Mo's soft call came from beyond the doorway.

He pulled himself upright, dropped the curtains and squared his shoulders.

The thought of walking back into that room, seeing the two people who had the power to move him so easily, there together, looking like forever, was like a fantasy come true. But it was his worst nightmare, too, because it *wasn't* forever. That was the reality of the situation. In a short time, this would all be over. Bev would be back with her mother, a situation he was powerless to stop. Mo would be gone, off looking for the man who could give her what she really wanted. And he was powerless to stop that, too.

The thought of her lying in another man's arms, waiting for some other man to empty his passion-filled body into her own, was maddening. It made him angry—at Mo, at the unknown stranger, at himself.

Gabriel closed his eyes and drew his hands into fists, pushing away his anger, forcing himself not to think, so that he could face whatever he'd find in the other room.

When he finally stepped back into the room he saw that Bev was up, rubbing her eyes, staring around as though she'd just awakened in Oz.

"Where's Winnie?" she demanded.

Mo eased her arm back from Bev's shoulder. "She's gone home to her own bed, which is where you should be right now," she whispered to the girl, her eyes meeting Gabe's across the room, welcoming him back. "I didn't know you were such a storyteller," she told him, her smile lighting up the green of her eyes.

"I'm not," he admitted. "But I was once a boy, and I'd wager that Josh and Sam are not all that finicky about their stories."

"You're right," she said, rising to her feet and pulling Bev's weary little form up beside her as she grasped her under the arm to keep the girl standing. "They mostly like the attention. But," she added, as she began to slowly lead Bev toward the staircase, "it was still a good story. The princess wasn't a shy, retiring mouse like she might have been if someone else had been making it up. And I liked the part about the cookie crumbs. Kind of a Gabriel Bonner personal touch, I'd say."

Mo paused at the bottom of the stairs, glancing back over her shoulder at Gabriel. The soft cotton of her dress was bunching up higher than she probably realized with Bev's body limply pushing at the material. She was holding Bev up by sheer will and was smiling at him as if he had just gone out and slain a dragon for her instead of merely entertaining her cousin's children with a foolish fairy tale. There was admiration in her eyes, and as he stepped closer he detected that small, nearly imperceptible catch in her breathing that he was beginning to anticipate—to need—in his life. He needed to know that his presence bothered her, that she desired him. He needed her to look at him that way more often.

Quickly Gabriel jerked his body up straight. He was starting to fantasize on his feet just from the force of the woman's smile. Good God, he was losing it completely.

"Let me take her. She's not that light anymore. You shouldn't be doing that," Gabriel said, his voice stiff and cool as he swung Bev high into his arms and started up the stairs at a too rapid pace.

Aware that Mo hadn't followed, that his words had been clipped and nearly angry, he wondered what she would be thinking.

At the first landing he turned and looked down at her. She was watching him, wary, worried.

"Was the evening so awful?" she asked, her tone laced with sympathy. She lowered her eyes, playing with the knob at the end of the banister.

If he hadn't been holding Bev, Gabe would have been downstairs in a minute. Mo's voice was so filled with uncertainty.

"They're nice kids," he assured her. "It was a good evening. You made it easy for me. You—" He forced himself to say the next words. "You'll make a good mother someday, when you have children of your own."

The smile that he was waiting for never materialized. Instead she studied him, silent and still. Her eyes met his, deep green orbs that drew his breath from him and caused him to shake inside. They both knew that her children would not be his. The pain in Gabriel's throat made breathing nearly impossible.

A tiny yawn broke the stillness. Bev struggled and tried to sit upright in Gabriel's arms. Then she craned her neck, turning to Mo at the bottom of the stairs.

"'Night, Mo," she said, her voice drowsy and contented. "I love my nails." She studied them blindly for Gabe could see that her eyes weren't really focused. She fell back into her father's arms as she continued talking. "Mo's fun, daddy. Why can't she just stay here forever?"

It was the question Gabe had been struggling to avoid all night long. And it had taken a child's simplicity and directness to give life to the words he would have never spoken.

But as his daughter began to relax into dreamland once again, Gabriel didn't have to look up to know that he needn't answer that too tough question. Bev was almost asleep . . . and Mo had already disappeared into the depths of the house.

In spite of her magical vanishing act the night before, Mo appeared again the next morning. She'd given Gabriel her word that she would do her best by him and Bev, and she was determined not to let her personal feelings get in the way of any promises she had made.

As she moved through the days ahead, Mo struggled to keep her attention focused only on Bev, trying not to notice

Gabriel too much. Doing so might only remind her of Bev's innocent question: Why couldn't she stay forever?

But at night, exhausted as she was from the day's activities, Mo couldn't keep her thoughts at bay. In the deepest hours before dawn, the question echoed through her mind, over and over. But it was her own voice plaintively appealing to Gabriel.

Why can't I stay with you forever?

She always woke up before Gabriel could answer, and Mo knew it was because she was afraid of what his answer would be.

She had her own reasons for not wanting to push into a relationship, and he had his. But voicing general, practical platitudes about a person's reasons for remaining single and carefree was one thing. Having a man personally reject you was another. Having him reject you in your nightmares was nearly as bad, Mo figured. And at the moment, she didn't want to try out the experience just to see if she was right.

She didn't want to know what came after the passion had flared and been spent, when the glaring light of morning reared its ugly head on reality. She couldn't let herself face the kind of pain that could cripple her emotions for life.

So she moved about, writing at night, smiling throughout the day, throwing herself into the joys that children always brought with them, playing games, singing songs, slopping up the kitchen with Bev as they cooked and painted and experimented with their nails. She tried to pretend that Gabriel was just another big kid. Which was, of course, impossible.

He made it impossible.

When she held paste-covered hands out at her sides the day they'd made a piñata, he grabbed a soapy cloth, running it over her palms, washing away the goo with a touch so slight that another person might have barely felt it. Mo's nerves vibrated with every slow circle of the cloth.

When she twirled around, showing Bev the swirl of the skirt she'd attempted to make, Mo looked up to find Gabriel lodged in the doorway, his smoky blue eyes making her too aware of just how high her skirt had flared about her bare legs.

And then one day when Mo was following Bev into the house, supremely conscious of the snug fit of her shorts against her bottom as Gabriel came up behind her, the slamming of a car door in the driveway brought her spinning around.

At first Mo thought the woman might be Nora. The ice-blue dress, the sheer stockings on perfect legs, the delicate bone structure, all spoke of class and sophistication. But Mo remembered the picture in Bev's room. This was not Gabriel's ex-wife.

"It's Patrice," Bev informed her as Gabriel stepped forward to meet the woman. "I've met her once or twice. She's . . . a friend of Dad's."

"We should go inside," Mo urged, placing a hand on Bev's shoulder and steering her toward the door. The little girl hung back and Mo continued into the house herself. She remembered the pictures in the paper. She had nearly forgotten. In the midst of all the foolish, simple activities they'd been engaging in for the past few days, Mo had nearly forgotten that Gabriel was, in fact, a society kingpin. He was a man about town, single, handsome and . . . eligible. He had dated the woman standing by the shiny red sports car outside. He had . . . touched her in the same ways that he'd touched Mo not so long ago.

The thought sent her plunging into the house, to hide from her thoughts, to lose herself in mindless activity.

When Gabriel came back into the house, Mo had already excused herself and made her way to the laundry room. She was ironing, a job she'd always considered a royal pain.

"I got that shirt back from the cleaners yesterday," he offered in that husky voice that always did unspeakable things to her insides.

"They forgot a wrinkle."

"Are we going to sue, or will you be satisfied with simply beating my shirt to death?" Gabriel asked as she pummeled the white linen with the heavy metal of the steam iron. She could feel his smile, but she refused to look up.

"It's important for an executive to always look his best, at all times," she emphasized. It was a line borrowed from Richard, who'd carefully explained that having a throwback to the flower-child era as a wife didn't exactly fit the corporate image.

"And you think I don't pass muster?" Gabriel asked incredulously. "You'd like me to change my appearance?"

He was moving closer now, his seductive voice drifting over her, drugging her the way it always did. She might be all right if she didn't look into his eyes . . . or if he didn't get too near.

"I—I didn't mean it that way. You know very well that you look—"

Wonderful, the voice inside her head said. *Sexy,* the voice went on. *Mouth-watering,* it continued.

Enough, Mo told the voice.

"You look fine," she finished, looking up at him indignantly.

His smile would have melted any other woman's heart in a nanosecond, but Mo told herself she was made of sterner stuff. She could resist the endearing crinkles at the corners of his eyes, the warm, male scent of him as he took another step and stopped by her side.

"Mo..." Gabriel crooned. "You're such a flatterer. Why have you stashed yourself away again? There was someone who wanted to meet you."

Mo could feel her eyes rounding at his words. She knew who Patrice Munroe was, and she couldn't imagine any reason why the woman would want to meet a second-rate housekeeper.

As usual, Gabriel read her expression too easily. His smile broadened, his dimples appeared. "She's read your work," he explained. "I think she wanted an autograph."

"She came here for my autograph?" Mo couldn't keep the disbelief from her voice.

"Well, not exactly." Gabriel had the grace to look sheepish. "But she seemed very interested in what you did for a living. And—"

"And she gave Dad her invitation to the ball because she's going to be out of town." Bev had appeared in the doorway, doing a dance on her toes. Her eyes were bright, snapping with enthusiasm. "You're going to go, aren't you, Mo?"

Mo looked up at Gabriel, surprised to see a dark flush spreading over his face.

"Sorry, I'm up to my bangs in ironing," Mo said, knowing full well that whatever this was all about, Gabriel didn't intend to ask his housekeeper to a ball. Even a housekeeper that he wouldn't mind crawling into bed with.

"Oh, no, Mo! You've got to go!" Bev did a slow twirl around the small space of the laundry room. "It's so neat. I remember when Mom used to go. You get to dress up like Cinderella and everything."

Her final spin sent her too near Mo's ironing board and Mo reached out to stop her, but Gabriel had already caught Bev by the arm, halting her progress.

Leaning over the board, Mo found herself nose to nose with Gabriel.

"I *would* like for you to go," he said softly.

"My tiara's in the shop," Mo whispered.

"You don't need a tiara, Mo," Bev insisted indignantly, wiggling free of her father's grasp. She was hopping around again, an accident waiting to happen.

Mo tugged the iron's cord from the electrical socket and moved it out of Bev's way.

"Tell her she doesn't need a tiara, Daddy," Bev begged.

Gabriel rubbed one hand through his hair. "She knows that, cupcake," he explained.

"But—"

"I'll keep trying," he promised. "You go on up to your room and draw some dress designs for your dolls. I'll work on Mo. All right?"

Bev contemplated that suggestion for a minute. "Would you let me design a dress for Mo? That would be so neat!" She flashed her father an encouraging smile and skipped over to the door. "Don't worry," she told Mo as she hung back for a moment. "Dad's a good dancer. Even Mom says so."

When she was gone, Mo reached for the cord on her iron, but Gabriel placed his hand over hers.

"Sorry about that," she told him.

"About what?"

"Well, about this whole ball thing. I'll explain it all to Bev in the morning."

Gabriel placed one finger under Mo's chin, forcing her to look up into the blue depths of his eyes. "And what will you tell her?" he asked.

"That you're not taking me to the ball."

"You wouldn't want to go with me?"

Mo could swear she heard pain in Gabriel's voice. Which was foolish, of course. The man could take any woman he wanted. She shook her head in frustration. "Don't tell me you came in here to invite me to a party. You didn't, did you?"

He shook his head slowly, folding his fingers gently around her chin, rubbing her jaw with his thumb. "I'll be damned if I know exactly why I came in here," he whispered. "But it seems like an awfully good idea to me, even if I didn't think of it myself."

"Then you must not be thinking very clearly right now."

She tried to push his hand away, but he dipped his head, dropping a feather-light kiss on her cheek.

"Shhh," he soothed. "And you're right. I'm not thinking very clearly right now. Are you?"

Mo was barely breathing, much less thinking—but she was trying to. "You can't take your housekeeper to an important social function."

He lowered his head and touched his lips to her throat, kissing his way back up to her mouth. When he slid his hands up her sides and around to cup the fullness of her breasts, Mo closed her eyes and leaned into him, raising one arm to loop it around his neck.

"Why can't I take you?" he whispered against her lips.

With his fingers gently stroking back and forth, she couldn't think. She didn't know. "Because," she said lamely, swallowing at the sensation of his lips moving against her skin, coaxing her to forget all rational thought.

Because. Because here in this house, she could pretend *sometimes*—not often, but *sometimes*—that things would work out all right. But out there, in Gabriel's world, the truth would be all too evident. Out there where all the Patrice Munroes existed, she'd be nervous, she'd make mistakes. He'd see once and for all that while she might do as a housekeeper, maybe even as a lover, she would never do as anything else. She would never quite fit. And she couldn't risk the pain of trying. She didn't do those things anymore. She didn't take those types of risks, because she knew how it would end.

Pushing away, she forced herself to look into his eyes. "I don't want to go," she told him. "I don't like those kinds of things."

"You don't want to go, or you don't want to go with me?" He had slipped his fingers to her shoulders, and she could feel his grip tighten with the tension of the moment.

The question hung between them. Mo tried to make herself tell Gabriel the lie that would put an end to the subject once and for all. She opened her mouth to speak, but she couldn't force the words from her throat, not with his beautiful, worried face so close to hers, not when he was still touching her....

In the distance, it seemed, almost from another planet, the ringing of the phone broke the silence.

Mo dropped her head.

Gabriel removed his hands from her shoulders.

With the second ring, Mo took a deep breath and brushed her hair back from her face.

Gabriel straightened his tie and gave her an apologetic glance as he walked to the phone.

When he came back he was still pulling at his tie.

Mo looked at him expectantly, reading his tension as easily as she could read her own mind.

"It was Nora," he said, his voice flat and too quiet. Much, much too quiet. "She and Harry are back. They've got his parents with them. And Nora wants Bev to come meet them before they return to Florida at the end of the week. She wants her back...tomorrow night."

All thoughts of her disagreement with Gabriel flew away like fluttering sparrows. Mo felt his denial, immediate, intense. The thought that was running through her head just wouldn't be silenced. "But it's two days early," she whispered, listening to her own protest.

Gabriel tersely nodded his agreement. "So how do I tell her, Mo? What kind of a father am I?" he asked quietly.

"How can I send my child away so easily, just because someone tells me to?"

Mo shook her head, her eyes blurring so much that Gabriel's face nearly disappeared. But she heard the deep, painful breath he took. When she blinked, she saw him swallow, clenching his fists, trying to control his reaction. In spite of whatever warnings had gone off in her head only moments before, Mo couldn't stop herself now from answering his question in the only way she could.

Walking to Gabriel, she laced her arms around his waist, pressed her already damp cheek to his chest. "*We'll* tell her," she promised. "*We'll* help her."

Leaving the room in silence, they climbed the stairs, their steps slowing as they neared Bev's room.

She was singing inside, humming in the places where she had forgotten the words.

Gabriel froze at the sound. His grasp on Mo's fingers was bruising as he turned to her. "It breaks her heart every time we go through this," he said, his voice as cold as stone.

Mo touched his cheek, smoothing her fingers down to his lips. "And yours," she said, tracing the seam of his mouth.

His eyes pools of anger, Gabriel clutched her to him, kissing her quickly, then letting her go.

The act of touching her seemed to fuel his determination. "All right, let's get it over with. Now," he said, raising his hand to knock on the door. "While I'm able to halfway hide my true feelings. While I can still act like everything's okay."

"I'm here beside you," she agreed, grasping his hand.

And she was, beside him all the way, as he walked into that room, like a man whose legs had turned to lead.

Gabriel only looked once at Bev, but it was enough. In spite of deep breaths and determination, he hadn't been able to hide his emotions that quickly. The little girl knew, Mo could tell.

Bev launched herself into her father's arms, curling her arms around his neck like tenacious vines fearful of being pulled away from their anchor.

"I don't want to go yet." Her sobs began quietly, then grew, racking her slender body, making her shake with misery as Gabriel spoke softly and caressed her back, trying to soothe when there was no comfort to be had.

Mo pressed her hands to her lips, knowing now, at last, why Gabriel would never have another child.

Chapter Eight

It should be raining today, Mo thought, as she trudged down the stairs the following morning at dawn's first light. It was the day Bev was going home, and it felt like the skies should have responded with a gloom-and-doom cloud cover.

But the sun was creeping higher every minute, pouring golden buckets of light over everything in sight. Mo pulled back the curtains to let the glow inside, remembering other times when she'd been down, when her father had criticized her, failed to notice her, sent her spiraling into sadness. And how she'd always turned her face to the light with the help of sunshine, Aunt Rose and her own fierce determination to come out on top.

Well, today it was her turn to help someone else get over the dark places. She wasn't sure that there was much she could do, but Mo knew she had to try.

By the time Bev and Gabriel arrived downstairs, there was hot coffee and glasses of orange juice waiting. There were doughnuts frying in a pan, heavy and fragrant and loaded with the type of richness reserved for the most special of occasions.

Mo lifted the doughnuts out of the pan one by one, placing them on a plate. She sprinkled them with sugar and cinnamon, then turned to Gabriel.

"I stuffed a backpack with some snacks, a camera and a few other necessities. You never made it to the zoo," she reminded him, sliding a mug of coffee and a full pot of cream to him.

Gabriel raised his head to look at her, his face showing the strain of the night before. But his smile was sincere and it touched at the shadows in his eyes.

"You'll come?" he asked, looking at Mo as he reached out to stroke Bev's hair, a gesture Mo was sure he wasn't even aware of.

"No, not today," she answered, as if there would be a tomorrow.

"Come with us, Mo," Bev said, and Mo couldn't ignore the joy that filled her. After all, Gabriel was an adult, one who observed all the polite rules of society. But Bev was a child, and children usually followed their hearts.

Still Mo shook her head. "This time's for you and your dad. Besides, I have a special something planned for when you get back, and I need time to get things ready."

"What is it?" Bev asked, her eagerness all that Mo could have wished for. Now, if that anticipation would only last a few hours more, if Mo's plans lived up to Bev's expectations, she'd know that Gabriel's daughter would remember this last day with fondness instead of sadness.

At least, that's what she hoped for, Mo thought, as she watched Bev march upstairs to get ready.

Gabriel only waited for the closing of the door before he caught Mo around the waist and swung her into his arms.

"You," he announced, sliding his hands up her sides to frame her face, "are a miracle worker. I would have sworn nothing could have brought a smile to my daughter's face today."

Mo didn't even try to pull back this time. She was where she wanted to be. And like Bev, she still had a little time left.

"I just wanted her to remember this day as a happy one," she reasoned. "What better way to do that than plan a surprise?"

"And I suppose you're not going to tell me what it is," he said, running his thumb over Mo's lips.

She surprised *herself* by wrapping her arms about his waist. Today wasn't a day for holding back or following the rules. Tomorrow would be soon enough.

"You suppose right," she said softly. Standing on her toes, she placed her lips against his. "A surprise is no fun if you tell what it is," she whispered.

"To repeat your own words, I'm not a child," he whispered back, moving his hands to her hair, angling his mouth to fit her own.

Mo would never argue the truth of those words, and she reveled in the feel of the man in her arms. He was warm and hard...and hungry for something other than food.

Without thought, her lips parted, as Gabriel deepened the kiss, dragging her tightly against him. She pressed herself closer to him, as close as she could get, moving her hands over the muscles in his back. For this moment she could hold him as if she'd never let her go. For this instant she could pretend forever was possible. Mo had always been good at pretending—it was how she made her living—but she had never wanted to make believe as much as she wanted to now.

Still, make-believe always ended, and eventually Gabriel loosened his grip on her, pulled back to look into her eyes. Mo could hear the sound of Bev's soft footsteps on the stairway.

"You're always a surprise to me, Mo," Gabriel told her. "Always."

"But you're not quite sure you like surprises, are you?" she asked, with sudden conviction.

"I haven't ever been very good at dealing with them," he confessed. "I like to have my own hand on the controls. At least, I always have."

"Then I'll bet you're a little nervous right now. Worried about what I have planned?" she teased, raising her brows exactly the way Gabriel did when he was teasing her.

"No. I'm not worried about your plans." Gabriel ran one finger along the delicate skin of Mo's jawline as Bev slid into the room and pronounced herself ready. "I have absolute faith in you."

It was the first time Mo could remember anyone ever saying those words to her.

Gabriel strolled through the zoo with Bev, noting her somewhat muted enthusiasm at their day in the wind and the sun. He was grateful that she hadn't yet gotten too sophisticated to feel embarrassed about holding his hand from time to time, and he concentrated all his attention on her and on their last day together. All his attention except for the thoughts he was directing toward Mo, that is.

Mo was a wonder and a puzzle to him. She'd been genuinely saddened to hear that Bev was leaving, and she'd devoted herself to making this day special for his child, a child that wasn't even hers. A child she obviously cared about.

And in less time than he wanted to acknowledge, Mo would be gone, too. Like Bev.

"Dad, you're not looking at the monkeys," Bev admonished, running around to stand in front of him, her small arms folded in frustration.

He grinned and ran his index finger down the length of her small nose. "How could I miss the monkeys?" he teased.

"Your mind was wandering," she said, tapping her toe on the ground. Then she sighed. "Mine was, too."

"I know," he said, bending down to look her in the eye. "You didn't even roar at the lions like you always do." Gabriel deliberately smiled to let her know that he was onto her.

"Daddy, I'm too old to do that now," Bev warned. Then, looking around at the crowds of people passing by, she went on, as though she'd already forgotten her slight indignation. "I know you love the zoo," she admitted. "But this isn't really that much fun today, is it?"

"You're bored?"

"No. Just thinking. You were, too. About Mo."

"You caught me," he said with a shrug, turning his palms up in resignation. "Are you mad at me?"

"No-o-o," she drawled. "No. She's nice, isn't she?"

Nice. What a simple word. It hardly began to describe his feelings for Mo. But those feelings weren't for sharing with Bev. Not now.

"She's nice," he finally agreed.

Suddenly Bev tipped her head back and grinned wickedly. "We could go home."

"Bev," Gabriel admonished, taking her hand and starting to walk. "You know that Mo's planning a surprise. We haven't even been gone an hour."

"But you don't like surprises," she reminded him. "I heard you tell her so."

"Okay, you got me there," he said, turning down the lane that led toward the exit. "But Mo does."

"Yeah, she does," Bev said, biting her lip. "I guess it wouldn't be nice to spoil her surprise, would it?"

"What do you think?"

"I think maybe you're right." Bev's sigh was long and drawn out. "All right, we still haven't seen the giraffes. Or the bears."

"That's my Bev," Gabriel soothed. "Think they have any new cubs?"

"Maybe," she answered, obviously resigned to her fate. "How long do you think Mo's going to be, Dad?"

Gabriel wished he could answer that question. In more ways than one. If there was something that was becoming more and more clear to him, it was that Mo had crept into his life and changed it. He wanted her, and soon she'd be gone, unless . . .

Gabriel couldn't finish that thought. All he knew was that it was a very big *unless* for a man who didn't make hasty decisions.

The house was covered in streamers. The formerly white-on-white living room was filled to overflowing with balloons in shades of plum, hot pink and tangerine. Mo had found the box of photos she'd discovered and covered the walls with prints of Bev and Gabriel and Nora, and even some of Bev's gaudy manicure, the ones she'd rushed to the one-hour photo-finishing shop. She'd made a cake, a trifle lopsided for the hurry. Spelled out in pink and orange and lavender sprinkles, were the words *For Bev.*

When Gabriel opened the door, Bev squealed her delight, running in to look at herself and her father in poses of days gone by. Mo had purposely concentrated on the silliest pictures she could find, ones designed to make Bev and Gabriel howl at themselves and wonder how anyone had ever managed to catch them with their mouths hanging open or their eyes squeezed tightly shut.

"You work fast," Gabriel said, coming up to lean over Mo's shoulder and whisper in her ear. "I like it."

"And to think I wanted to come back before you were done," Bev admitted.

Mo widened her eyes in mock surprise, and Bev shrugged. "Dad said we had to wait until you were ready."

"Well, I'm not quite done," Mo said slyly. "There's a picnic basket I didn't bring in yet. And one other thing."

"What other thing?" Bev demanded.

Mo's only answer was a smile, but she slipped from the room and returned, pushing a squeaking cart.

Gabriel took one look and groaned.

"Mo," he warned. "Those old home movies? You wouldn't punish me this way...."

She placed her hands on her hips and smiled, stepping nearer to him, the electrical cord dangling from her fingers. "Oh, come on, Gabriel, it'll be fun. Here, plug this in. And close the curtains."

"It won't be fun. What it will be is humiliating. You can't know—"

"What you looked like as a skinny kid wearing boxer shorts? Oh, yes I can. I already previewed all the reels. For Bev's sake, of course."

Gabriel's answering moan almost undid Mo. She wondered if he was really embarrassed. That hadn't been her intent.

Leaning close, she stood on her toes and whispered near his ear. "I took that one out, in case you're worried. But you were kind of cute."

Gabriel growled and sighed his resignation. "All right, Mo, let's get this torture over with." But she noticed that he smiled as he said it.

Ninety minutes later, the clock struck two. Mo looked at Gabriel across the room.

He nodded back at her, his face suddenly sober.

For the last hour and a half, they'd stuffed themselves with pizza and cake and soft drinks. They'd giggled at the movies Mo had unearthed from a dusty shelf in one of the guest-room closets.

Bev had teased Gabriel about his boyish clowning for the camera and Gabriel had tickled Bev when she'd hinted that his ears had been big. They'd laughed until they cried, and then watched some more.

But now the clock had cut into their reverie.

Bev was staring at a picture on the wall.

"Could I take this with me?" she asked Mo, pointing to a picture of the three of them. Josh's brother Mike had taken it the day before, and it was slightly crooked, a trifle out of focus.

"I meant for you to take them with you," Mo said, picking up a photo of Bev in her droopy hat sitting next to Gabriel. She gathered the few remaining prints together, then moved to the door. "Why don't I pack some of your things while you and your dad finish up here?" she suggested.

And suddenly the room seemed drab and gloomy in spite of the colored streamers and balloons, in spite of the sunshine that had slipped in as soon as Mo turned off the projector and opened the curtains.

She wandered up the stairs to where Bev had already started putting out her clothes.

Slowly, Mo began to fold and push things into the waiting suitcase.

The tiny creak of the door brought her head up. Gabriel was standing in the doorway.

Mo looked at him, a question in her eyes.

"She went down the street to say goodbye to a friend," he explained.

Mo nodded, but didn't look away.

"You're packing her poodle," he said, the question in his voice.

"Darn right I am," she said, trying to keep her voice steady. "Harry doesn't know beans about kids. Harry is a skunk, I think." Mo knew she shouldn't have said that, so she continued packing clothes and kept her eyes on her task.

Gabriel stepped around the bed, catching Mo's hands in his own. "Harry is a skunk," he agreed, bringing her fingers to his lips. "And you're an angel."

Mo looked up at him through eyes that were as bright and damp as his own. "Angels don't call people names," she corrected.

"They must," he disagreed. "Because I just heard you call Harry a name, and not a very nice one, either."

"I can't help it," Mo defended herself. "It's so obvious that he doesn't know the first thing about the way little girls feel." She tried to look away, to hide her distress, knowing that he was even more upset than she was. Bev was his daughter, after all. But Gabriel slipped his fingers beneath her chin and raised her face to his.

"If I could go back in time and change the way your father was, I would, sweetheart," he told her.

She shook her head slowly, not leaving the comfort of his touch. "You don't have to. Just be a good father to Bev."

His nod was just as slow. "I try—I *do* try."

Her look of sadness turned into a grimace at his words. "I didn't mean that the way it sounded. I know you try. And you succeed. You're a wonderful father." *You're a wonderful man,* she wanted to say.

But she didn't. Instead she simply closed the suitcase and pushed it into his hand. "You'd better go to her now. She'll need you."

And Mo stood alone, watching him go, knowing that finally Gabriel had to face his loss. She couldn't throw a party to pretend away the pain that they all had to face this time.

It was as if the sun moved to St. Paul the day Bev went back home. Gabriel grew quiet and thoughtful. He was gone a lot, away at the office, making up for the hours he'd missed, Mo supposed.

She found herself alone, with only her computer for company, a social arrangement she'd once deemed ideal. Now she sat there feeling dull and void of ideas. She spent her hours cleaning rooms that no one ever frequented and plunking out stories that no one would ever publish.

And she listened for Gabriel as he wandered the house late at night, unaware of her presence.

She hadn't felt this far away from him even when they'd first met. She missed him with a bittersweet longing she'd never felt before. It was a frightening thought, a pale hint of what the future would bring.

One morning as Mo dragged herself around the kitchen, cleaning up the remains of her simple breakfast, she looked up to find Gabriel standing inside the doorway. He was holding a letter in his hand ... and he was smiling ... at her.

Welcome back to Chicago, Mo thought, glancing out the window at the rising sun.

"Bev?" she asked, putting down the plate she'd just picked up.

Gabriel nodded. He rubbed his jaw. "She's settling in again a bit, I think. At any rate, she gave me strict orders. I'm to tell you that her mother nearly croaked when she saw the picture of her baby wearing those 'hideous fingernails.' But Nora also said she'd take her to do it again someday if she keeps her grades up."

Mo felt the corners of her lips lifting and gave a sigh of relief. Smiling hadn't been on her agenda lately. But it *was* good to know that Nora had her lighter side.

"What else did she say?" Mo coaxed, watching the way Gabriel slid the letter into his shirt pocket as though it were a treasure map.

He gave his pocket a tap. "Oh, a lot of rather bossy stuff. My daughter likes to give me advice from time to time, you understand."

He was grinning from ear to ear.

The effect of Gabriel's smile was instantaneous. Mo's heart began to do a quick tap dance inside her chest. If she jumped off the table right now, she was sure she could fly like Peter Pan—without the fairy dust.

"Oh, admit it," she said, picking up the sugar bowl and stashing it on a shelf. "You love every single bossy comment she makes."

Gabriel shrugged, lifting his hands in an admission of defeat. "Hey, what can I say? Good advice is good advice. And sometimes Bev's insight surprises me."

Mo waited for him to expand on that comment, tracing her thumb around the rim of an empty coffee cup. But when Gabriel remained silent and secretive, she moved to the sink and began to run warm water.

"When do you think she'll be back again?" she asked.

"I don't know. I haven't talked to Nora yet," he said, coming up behind Mo and placing the rest of the dishes on the counter.

Though she pretended interest in her chores, Mo knew that it was Gabriel's closeness that held her attention. He hadn't come near her in days.

"She'll be back one day soon." His quiet voice drifted through the sunshine-filled kitchen. Moving behind her, he rested his cheek on her hair. "But not for long. Never long enough."

Sucking in a great gulp of air, Mo shivered when Gabriel wrapped his arms about her, just beneath her breasts. "But—but she will be back," Mo whispered.

"Yes, and then she'll be gone again. She always goes. But she does always come back. Somehow we survive."

But, Gabriel thought, breathing in the fresh-washed scent of Mo's hair, Mo wouldn't be back once she was gone. He wondered how he would survive without her. He'd gotten through his loss of Bev before because she *would* always be back, always be his little girl. But what about Mo?

These last few days, he'd thought of little else. Mo had gotten to him, made him want her, and worse, made him care for her.

He practically had to sit on his hands when she was around. He wanted to make her his own in truly elemental ways. He wanted to strip away those unintentionally seductive clothes she wore and feel her bare flesh against his own, to feel the difference between her soft breasts and the peaks of her nipples as he moved above her, to grasp her hips in his hands as he prepared to sheathe himself inside her. But...

Gabriel's thoughts always went haywire at that point. She wasn't a woman he could take casually. She was more than that. And if he had her, he'd want her for more than a day or two, for more than the kind of uninvolved relationship she claimed to be looking for.

The question was, could he ask for more? And if he did, could he reciprocate with what she needed? Could he ever offer her a child?

Tough questions, and not the kind a man like him could answer overnight. Gabriel had been trying for days, possibly for weeks, maybe since the day he'd met her. He wondered if he would ever have the answer, if he'd ever have Mo.

He didn't know. He only knew that he wanted to try, to test the waters. But this time he'd go slowly, sweetly, sensibly. He wouldn't rush in and make any irrevocable decisions. But he would make a move, make a conscious decision. He'd been touching her for weeks against his will. Now he was going to think first—and then he'd touch her. Not just her body. But her heart, he hoped. That was the plan—no rushing in, no getting in over his head. Just slow and practical and controlled, so that he could turn back before things got out of hand. If he had to.

"Gabriel?" Mo's breath was soft against the skin of his arm, and he realized that he'd been holding her, silently, for more time than could possibly be considered sensible. "Are you going in to work today? Or... not?"

The sound of her voice humming its way through his body, the feel of the soft slope of her breast just touching his arm, the need to turn and run his hands over her made his senses ignite.

"Work?" he asked, pulling his arms away as if she were a match that had burned down to his fingertips. "Yes," he said suddenly. "I'm going. God, yes. I guess I'd better get going now."

Mo watched him turn from her quickly, but not before she saw the tension that transformed his face into stiff planes, his jaw into granite. These past few days had been hard for him. Very hard, she knew.

In spite of the letter, he was still missing Bev as he always would, and Mo had never felt so helpless to ease his distress and to bring the smile back to his eyes.

If there was only some way to bring Bev back. Maybe there was a way to get Nora to move back to Chicago. But of course, Nora had Harry. In a recent letter, she'd told Gabriel that she and Harry were seriously considering getting married. And Harry might well be the key... if Harry decided that Chicago had something that would draw him.

Wandering into her room, Mo perused her shelves, nervously playing with the top button on her blouse. What would attract a man like Harry? He was a salesman, Bev had said. What could Mo do to sell a salesman on a city?

She took a deep breath and closed her eyes. In the years she'd been writing, she'd become quite a researcher. She'd used her skills to seduce and inform her readers, to get them involved and win them over. Once she'd even written a few articles on the attractions of the city. They'd been mostly for tourists, but there was one that might be of interest to an enterprising salesman. The article had been written a while ago, but it was still timely. She hadn't gotten paid well for it at the time, she remembered, but it was a good piece. If she just dropped it in the mail for Harry... it might... it would be...

Interfering, her conscience told her. *Butting in.*

She tried to close her mind.

You said you wouldn't do this anymore, she heard that little voice inside her saying. *You weren't going to go out of your way for anyone else.*

But she saw Gabriel's eyes as they'd looked when he walked out the door this morning. She remembered Bev's tears the day she'd left her father to return home.

It wasn't interfering, and she wasn't doing this to further her own cause, Mo argued. She was doing this for Bev. She was doing this for Gabriel...not to try to make him love her, but because she cared about him, because she wanted to see him happy.

Mo knew now that she'd do anything she had to if it would bring Gabriel's happiness, his daughter, back to him.

Sitting down at her computer, she gathered her books and boxes about her. She pushed aside any lingering notions of risk and doom, and began to sift through the material until she found what she was looking for.

She read the article over. Once. Twice. She scribbled a note in the margin. And then another farther down the page. Then she read the article again.

Finally, satisfied with her update, she slipped it into an envelope, took a deep breath, closed her eyes. Then she hurried off and mailed the package to Harry before she could change her mind.

When she returned, she tuned out the last few hours, collapsing onto a cushy chair in the study, totally drained but satisfied, almost smug.

That's where Gabriel found her a short time later, flushed, exhausted, completely contented. She was munching on an Oreo and licking the crumbs from her lips.

When she looked up, Gabriel was smiling at her, clearly amused.

"What's funny?" she asked, holding out a cookie to him.

He shook his head and moved closer. "You are." His voice was low and husky. "Funny and sweet and tempting."

"Just discovered that, have you?" she asked, not trusting herself to be serious.

"No, I've known it for a long time. It just took my daughter to make me realize that I should do something about it."

Mo tilted her head, blinking as if her eyes, and not her ears, were the problem. "Bev told you to tell me that I was tempting?"

Gabriel's laugh touched Mo's heart. She'd missed it so much. "No, even Bev isn't that obvious. But she did remind me that I hadn't convinced you to go to the annual ball with me. And she gave me very explicit instructions on the type of dress I was to buy since she didn't have time to design it herself."

From behind him, Gabriel pulled out a package and laid it on Mo's lap.

"Would you? Would you consider it?" he asked. "Would you do me the very great honor of being my date for the ball?"

Mo looked at him, trying to tame her wayward impulse to simply say yes. She'd go anywhere with him.

She forced herself to swallow the words along with the last of the cookie crumbs. There had been other times, many times, when she'd been filled with excitement and enthusiasm. But when all was said and done, she'd returned home knowing that she'd somehow failed to make the grade.

She didn't set herself up for that kind of a letdown anymore.

But Gabriel had already moved to sit next to her. The scent of his cologne drifted around her; his thigh brushed her own. He took her hands in his, his thumbs rubbing small circles against her palms.

"Come with me, Mo," he urged with his magical smile, his too-seductive voice.

The blood thrummed through her fingers where he held them lightly. Mo could feel her heart start to beat faster...with anxiety and longing.

She knew the kind of women Gabriel escorted to such affairs. She also knew she wasn't one of them. She didn't fit the mold, or any mold she'd ever found. But this was Gabriel looking at her, coaxing her, waiting for her answer.

"I—I don't think this is exactly part of my job description," she told him breathlessly, taking the easy way out.

"An obvious oversight on my part," Gabriel said near her ear. "Just wait a minute and I'll pencil it in. Light housekeeping. Must waltz," he suggested.

Mo shook her head, finally smiling. "You're incorrigible. Try telling that to Aunt Rose."

Gabriel leaned back, his eyes wide with synthetic horror. "I may be incorrigible, but I prefer life without a rolling pin wrapped around my neck. Rose would never put up with such pompousness."

"And I would?" Mo looked him straight in the eyes, pretending indignity as she poked him in the chest with her index finger.

Gabriel caught her hand and brought it to his lips. "Probably not, but it was worth a try," he admitted. "Does this mean that you're turning me down?"

"Why me?" she whispered, studying his suddenly dark eyes. He could have asked anyone, a hundred women who were accustomed to such gatherings, who would fit right in without a hitch. She needed to know why he was asking her.

Gabriel drew her to her feet, his arms sliding beneath hers as he began to slowly move with her. "I thought we'd dance, Mo. I wanted to dance with you. I wanted to spend an evening with you. An entire evening."

Standing with her heart pressed to his, swaying in his arms, Mo felt her objections slip away. At that moment, Gabriel could have asked her to travel with him to an unexplored universe with no hope of return, and she couldn't have said no.

She'd been his housekeeper for weeks. She'd cooked for him, cleaned for him, shared with him and cared about him. But if her memory and Aunt Rose's last postcard served her right, the baby would arrive soon, and her time here would be gone. She'd be gone. She would never, ever again have the opportunity to simply be a *woman* in Gabriel's eyes, a woman who would stand by his side, dance in his arms and go home with him at the end of the evening.

She didn't even look at the dress still lying in its wrapper. Knowing Gabriel's taste in clothing, she was sure it was beautiful. But it could have been a rag, a sack, a single length of coarse burlap, and her answer would have been the same.

"I'll go with you, Gabriel," she promised. "I'll be your date for the dance."

She'd have her one night with Gabriel Bonner.

One night to look back on when her time here was done.

Chapter Nine

Mo's heart was sending out distress signals as she slipped the dress over her head. A simple, golden sheath which dipped low in the back, the gown was exquisite, clinging softly to her skin as it whispered its way down her body. But the appeal of the dress wasn't in its beauty, but in the knowledge that Gabriel had chosen it. Her nervousness didn't lie with the gown, but with the fact that soon she was going to walk out the door on Gabriel's arm. As his date. As the woman he had chosen to spend the evening with.

She was going to enter into a world of people who'd been born knowing they were impressive, who'd risen to the top of the social heap. Gabriel's friends. People who would see right through her.

Glancing into the mirror, Mo pulled her shoulders back and took a deep breath, reminding herself that she wasn't hoping to impress Gabriel. She just wanted to be with him. For one night. Her night.

If she fell on her face, that would be something she'd think about later, after she was gone. When it wouldn't matter.

"Liar," she told the mirror. She knew that in her heart she wanted to leave Gabriel with pleasant dreams of her. She also knew that she was about to break the promise she'd made to herself. For tonight she was going to do her darndest to impress Gabriel, to wow him, to be the woman of his dreams, a woman he'd like to take into his bed . . . his life.

But a light knock on her door made her tense immediately. She cleared her throat twice.

"Come in," she finally managed, and her voice was husky, too quiet.

She turned as Gabriel's body filled the doorway, her hand automatically moving to her throat.

He was dressed as she should have expected, in a black tux, his crisp white shirt accenting the tan that had deepened in the days he and Bev had spent outdoors. He looked like he'd been born in a tux, and she felt as if she'd been waiting to see him this way all her life.

Dredging up that slow, sensuous smile of his, Gabriel moved into the room. Mo swallowed at the gleam that came into his eyes. . . . He looked like a man who'd had a lot of women and who intended to have one more . . . tonight.

Gabriel nodded to where she still had her palm pressed against her throat. "Having second thoughts? Thinking of hiding out in the laundry room again tonight?"

His smile deepened, showing his dimples, and Mo instantly relaxed. She grinned up at him. "I would, but I can't seem to find another single item to wash or iron."

He held his palms out. "Maybe that's because I hid everything I could find. I didn't want to take a chance on letting you back out. Besides, I'm not sure I could take it if you started ironing my underwear. A man's got to draw the line somewhere.''

Mo felt the laugh climbing to her throat. She tilted her head. ''In the future, I'll try to exert restraint by remembering that you prefer your underwear rumpled.''

The laughter in Gabriel's eyes turned into a predatory glow and he took one step closer, placing his hand on her naked shoulder.

''Actually I'd prefer *your* underwear rumpled,'' he confided, bending to drop a kiss on the hollow of her throat where her own hand had been only seconds before. He peered down at her as though he were trying to see down her dress.

She wrinkled her nose at him. ''I think it's time for Cinderella to put in a call to her fairy godmother.''

He leaned even closer, his eyes wide with mock horror. ''Does that mean you're not wearing any underwear? I knew fairy godmothers were good at conjuring up something.''

''It means,'' she said, smiling sweetly and taking his arm, ''that it's time to haul the pumpkin out and be on our way.''

''I have a small confession to make, Cinderella. There are no pumpkins in my garden,'' he whispered in her ear. ''Unless you've put them there. But I can promise you this. I'll get you to the ball safely. You can send your fairy godmother on her way. I'll be the one watching over you tonight.''

That's exactly how Mo felt for the next short while: watched over, cherished.

Gabriel treated her with tenderness and care. He introduced her to his friends, but he didn't linger with them. She was the woman he'd come with, and Gabriel would do nothing to let her or anyone else forget that.

Not when she heard the not-so-quiet whispers of ''I wonder where Patrice is,'' not when people asked Gabriel where he and Mo had met.

"Mo graciously agreed to step in and help me when I lost my housekeeper. In her other life, she's a very talented writer. And a thoroughly good sport," he added for her ears alone.

"It's natural for people to be curious," she assured him when the tenth person had asked the same question and Gabriel was trying to apologize to her.

He shrugged as they moved on. "Most of them are very nice people. They've just never seen you before. You're like some sort of new exotic flower to them. Out of the ordinary."

"Like those people over there?" Mo said, nodding to where an elderly couple was making their way through the crowd. The woman bobbed along, encased in feathers from the top of her headpiece to the fluff on her shoes. The man was doing a slow rhumba across the floor, wearing a suit that was two sizes too small. Though a few people stopped to talk to them, Mo noticed that many turned aside when they drew near.

"The Peterbys—Lillian and Henry," Gabriel explained. "Henry used to have a dry cleaner before he lost it. Lillian... well, Lillian wears her feathers... always, everywhere. They show up now and then without invitations, and Henry rhumbas and tangos the night away. They are a bit eccentric. Most hosts find it easier to ignore them than to spoil the party by having them removed."

Eccentric. The word echoed through Mo's head along with the memory of a night when Richard had accused Mo of encouraging an "eccentric fool" to monopolize her time when important guests were present.

Eccentric. And the Peterbys didn't belong here any more than she did.

She touched Gabriel's arm. "Look how carefully he's supporting her, though," she said softly. "How she's smiling at him as though he rules the world."

Gabriel smiled down at her. "I said they hadn't been invited, Mo. I didn't say they weren't nice people. Mrs. Peterby was volunteering at the hospital one day when I had to take Bev in. I'll bet not many people here know that, or that Henry has a prizewinning rose garden. They're unusual but warmhearted. Come on, I'll introduce you later when they make their way around. And Henry will insist on teaching you to tango, if you don't already know how." He winked at her, grinning broadly.

"And you think I'll enjoy that, do you?" she asked, laughing up at him at the thought of stalking her way across the room and dipping low into chubby Mr. Peterby's arms.

"It's an experience not to be missed, I've heard," Gabriel assured her with relish, as the music began and he took her in his own strong arms. "He's actually very accomplished. Besides, you can teach *me* to tango later. I've got a strong urge to see what it's like to find myself bent over you with a rose clamped between my teeth."

"And will Mr. Peterby supply the rose?" she asked, widening her eyes.

"Undoubtedly. You deserve the best. I'm sure Henry will consider it an honor to have such a beautiful woman carrying one of his prize roses. You are very beautiful tonight, you know," he repeated, as he effortlessly spun her around the floor.

Mo was not nearly as accomplished a dancer as Gabriel. Nor had she ever learned how to gracefully accept such compliments. She could feel warmth invading her face as she looked to the side. "It's a lovely dress," she assured him. "Thank you."

Gabriel stopped dead in the middle of the dance floor, causing her to look up at him in alarm.

"That's better," he said when he had her attention, and he began to move to the music once more. "And it's not the dress I was talking about, Mo. You knew that. It didn't look one-tenth as good on the hanger as it does this minute. Without your body, your sparkle, that dress is nothing, but I'm absolutely positive that you, without the dress . . ." Gabriel groaned. "Lady, you without the dress . . . my mouth goes dry at the very thought."

Mo sucked in her breath, and Gabriel lifted her off her feet when she missed the next few steps.

He pulled her closer to him, leaning to whisper in her ear. "I haven't kissed you, Mo, not since we've been alone in the house, and I've wanted to. You know that."

"You've been away a lot," she choked out, swallowing hard.

"Damn right, I have," he agreed. "Because we'd both agreed that it wouldn't be wise for us to make love. To start something we couldn't finish. And I couldn't trust myself to stay in the house with you and not ask you to let me make love to you."

Mo nodded, unable to say more. She could feel her breasts starting to ache with his words. She could feel awareness growing low within her body.

"But I don't think I'm capable of being wise tonight, Mo," he told her. "I want you in my bed. I want to peel that dress off of you inch by inch. So if it's wisdom you're looking for tonight, you're going to have to do the thinking for both of us. You know I'll stop if you ask me to."

Biting her lip, Mo looked away. How could Gabriel know that any wisdom she might have ever had had flown away hours ago? She wanted him badly, too.

And he was expecting her to be wise?

When the music stopped, she followed him across the room, watching as he held her chair for her. At the candle-lit table she sat in the flickering light, watching the way Gabriel's dark jacket hugged the breadth of his shoulders, feeling the tingle of his fingers brushing hers when they clinked their glasses in a toast, seeing the way his eyes strayed to her wet lips after she'd taken a sip of wine.

This night was like magic she'd never known or had the knowledge to write about. She'd never had a man look at her like she was the ice cream that followed the cake, the oasis in the midst of a desert.

"You're enjoying yourself?" he asked, leaning toward her as he reached out to touch her hair.

"I'm glad I came," she agreed. "Better make this a permanent part of the job description. Aunt Rose might go for this."

"She's a party animal, all right, our Rose," Gabriel admitted with a grin. "But you're the one causing the stir tonight."

Mo nearly choked on her wine. "Oh, not a stir," she insisted. In her experience "causing a stir" had never been a positive experience.

As she reached for a soothing sip of water, a tall, blond giant stopped by Gabriel's side.

"Gabe," the man said, pounding Gabriel on the back. "Long time no see."

Gabriel looked up at him and nodded slightly. "Tom. It *has* been a long time." Then, when the other man only continued to stare at Mo, Gabriel sighed, turning to her as he made the necessary introductions.

"Maureen's a lovely name," Tom said, turning on the charm that had made him a legend among Gabriel's crowd.

Gabriel waited for Mo to tell the man just what *she* thought of the name Maureen. But she didn't.

"Would you consider leaving Gabe's side to dance with me for a while?" Tom smiled into Mo's eyes, his hand held out as though there could be no doubt of her answer.

Every muscle in Gabriel's body tensed. Tom Saynor was known for his tendency to sweep women out from under the noses of whatever man they were with. He was intelligent, he was of classic proportions, and his face— The man would probably have beautiful children when he got around to it.

The ugly thought reared its head just as Gabriel forced himself to smile encouragement at Mo. He wouldn't keep her chained to him, even though it was a thought he truly wanted to indulge at the moment. Tom was looking at Mo like she was a fresh chocolate éclair on a tray filled with stale doughnuts.

"I—I— That would be nice. Of course," Mo said, edging away from her seat. She cast one questioning glance back at Gabriel just before Tom pulled her into his engulfing embrace. Much closer than Gabriel had expected.

Tom's hand was touching Mo's bare back.

Immediately Gabriel had a change of heart about the wisdom of being so open-minded, of encouraging Mo to dance with any man who asked.

Her beautiful fiery curls were the perfect match for Tom's golden mane, Gabriel noted. And the man was certainly holding his head close enough to hers for anyone to see that easily enough. His lips were barely six inches from Mo's.

Gabriel was tempted to take out a ruler and measure. Just before he punched the guy right in the kisser that was inching steadily closer to Mo.

She's an adult, Gabriel told himself. *An intelligent, wise, wonderful woman who knows her own mind and knows how to take care of herself,* his thoughts continued. *And she's looking for someone to give her a child and then walk away. Are you willing to do that?*

Gabriel didn't know, but he was sure as hell that Tom Saynor and a dozen other men whose eyes had been turning to Mo all night would jump in to fill the breach in half a second if she looked at them. The thought of them waiting around like a wolf pack, fighting to be the man Mo would share her body with, nearly brought Gabriel to his knees.

With his eyes never leaving Mo, Gabriel knew the minute the man began to slide his hand up the exposed skin of her back.

Damn whatever caution he had left to the wind. Damn taking things slowly and sensibly. Damn waiting to tell her how he felt, to ask her if she'd have him. Caution meant sitting here waiting politely for Saynor or some other jerk to return her to his table. Gabe couldn't sit still that long.

He was not going to let Saynor or any other man try to start pawing her, try to take advantage of her, try to sneak into her soft body by offering her the baby that she wanted so badly.

No one was going to hurt her or use her. Even if he had to start an all-out brawl to keep it from happening.

Rising to his full height, Saynor in his sights, Gabriel began to thread his way purposefully through the maze of tables.

Mo was looking up at the blond head of the man who was holding her much too tightly. He was, she supposed, many women's idea of physical perfection. And he probably had most of the other attributes she'd remembered once telling Gabriel she was looking for in the man to father her child.

"Something wrong?" Tom said as he spun her around, pulling her even closer against him. Mo squirmed slightly, trying to free herself from his too tight embrace. She wondered why she didn't get that same warm rush of feeling for this man that she got whenever Gabriel held her. She *didn't* feel it. If she felt anything at all it was only... discomfort, possibly even revulsion.

"No, no, I'm fine," Mo said weakly, peering over his shoulder. There were other men watching them, their eyes speculative, questioning, as she drifted past them. Caught up in this man's arms as she was, she probably looked like a woman who was interested in more than a spin around the floor, Mo realized.

Pushing against her dance partner some more, she managed to find a little breathing room.

One man, she'd told her aunt. She was only looking for one man. Yet here she was in a room filled with eligible, attractive, intelligent men who were studying her with interest, and she couldn't find even one whose interest she could return.

But that wasn't true, Mo realized, as she searched the room for Gabriel. There *was* one man. There was *only* one man. There was only Gabriel. He was the reason she couldn't look at this man who held her. He was the reason she now knew she'd never have a child.

That sudden flash of reality nearly made her slip. She would never have a child, the child she'd longed for through the years. Because she loved Gabriel.

She loved him. She'd known it for a while, a long while, probably. And now she knew that she would never be able to act on her plans, after all. She could never lie with another man, hoping for a child, when Gabriel was the only man whose touch she desired. She would never ask Gabriel to be the man she'd been looking for. That had never been a possibility.

With that blindingly sad and clear insight, Mo came face-to-face with a truth she just couldn't avoid. She stopped moving, stepping back from the man who held her. "I'm sorry," she said with a sad smile.

Tom's eyes registered his confusion as Mo moved farther away.

In the distance, she saw Gabriel making his way across the dance floor. He looked like a warrior, ignoring the dancers he brushed against with his broad shoulders as he plowed through the crowd.

He was angry, Mo could see that. He'd probably seen her just the way those other men had, as a woman looking for the wrong thing. Hadn't Richard once accused her of laughing too loud, flirting when she didn't realize she had been?

But that had been Richard, a man who hadn't really mattered. This was Gabriel, the man she loved. And he was upset with her.

Or maybe not with her, Mo decided, seeing the way Gabriel's eyes strayed to Tom as though he wanted to burn the man to cinders with his glance.

Her spirits rising slightly, Mo turned to Tom, who was standing with a foolish expression on his face.

"You're...a wonderful dancer," she said, taking his hand and squeezing it. "But I don't think you and I should really dance any more right now. Gabriel—Gabriel is looking for me," she explained, turning away from him as she moved through the swaying crowd and walked right into Gabriel's arms.

"I guess he had to spread himself around," she explained with a small shrug as she put her arms around Gabriel and laid her cheek on his chest. "Would *you* dance with me again? Do you think that would be all right?"

Gabriel slipped his arms about her, bringing her closer than even Tom had held her. Mo squirmed, but only to get still closer.

"That would be more than all right, Cinderella," Gabriel told her, settling her right where she wanted to be, up against his heart. "That would be perfect."

He'd held Mo in his arms for most of the night, Gabriel realized, as they finally headed for home. He probably could have stayed like that forever. With Mo held close, he'd been hard-pressed to control his reaction to her, but he hadn't let her go, either. He hadn't made the fool mistake of letting another Tom Saynor get his hands on her. She hadn't even gotten to tango with Henry. And Gabriel felt a moment of regret. She would have enjoyed Henry. Next time, he promised.

Walking toward the car now, Gabriel swept his hand beneath her hair, touching the bare flesh beneath her curls. Her shiver brought him instant pleasure, as well as concern.

"You're not cold?" When she shook her head, joy passed through Gabriel's body. She wasn't cold, but she had shivered at his touch.

Suddenly Gabriel couldn't wait to get to the car. Turning her in his arms, he found her waist with his hands and lifted her up, near enough for her lips to touch his.

"The evening's not over," he said softly. It was a question more than a statement.

"No, it's early," she whispered, letting herself slide forward onto Gabriel's chest.

Her arms automatically found their home, twined round his neck, as she touched her lips to his.

Tonight, Mo knew, she wasn't Gabriel's housekeeper. She was his lady, his Cinderella. She couldn't try to hide behind the guise of her job this time. Nor did she want to hide.

"Come home with me," he urged, kissing her back as he turned them toward the car again.

Her laughter fell into the night like drops of honey come to life. "Of course," she said to his somewhat silly statement.

"You know what I mean," he replied, stopping once more. This time when he kissed her, he wasn't quick about it, but he was thorough. Bending her back over his arm, Gabriel traced his fingers down her cheek to her throat, then slid them lower still to the hollow between her breasts. "Come home with me, Mo," he whispered.

Mo swallowed and nodded, unable to speak for the longing in her throat. Tonight they wouldn't sleep in separate rooms. Tonight Gabriel would touch her in places he hadn't touched before. And she would touch him back, Mo promised herself.

But they wouldn't make a child. When Gabriel remembered this night, she wanted him to smile, with no regrets.

She wanted to smile. The tears for what she'd never have—forever with the man she loved and the child of her dreams—could come some other day.

As Gabriel pulled the car into the garage, Mo took a deep breath. It was as if all her life, all her dreams, hopes, aspirations had come down to this one night.

Suddenly, she wasn't sure if she was equal to whatever this evening would bring. She was afraid at once of disappointing and of knowing that she had disappointed.

"Don't worry," Gabriel said, leaning over to her, tilting her chin beneath her fingers. "I'm not looking for perfection, you know."

Her eyes opened wide and she tipped her head back, gazing into his eyes in the near darkness. "How did you know what I was thinking?" she whispered.

She could almost hear his smile as he touched one finger to the pulse point at her throat. "Your heart's pounding," he said simply. "Too hard for simple desire, I think." He dropped a kiss on the top of her head. "Besides, it was what *I* was thinking, that I wanted to please you so much that it scares me."

His comment was enough to break the tension that had enveloped the car for the last few miles home.

Wrapping her hand in his own, Gabriel led her toward the door and placed his key in the lock.

As he turned it, Mo heard a familiar sound from the hallway, that of the answering machine clicking on. And then Bev's voice. Urgent. Tearful.

"Daddy," she wailed into the phone. "Call me, please. Please call me." Her voice faded on a hiccup just as Gabriel made it through the door and grabbed up the receiver. But he was too late—Bev had already hung up.

As Gabriel redialed the number, Mo noted that there had been several other messages on the machine. An oddity this late at night.

She looked at him, questioning, and he shook his head.

Not knowing what else to do, Mo left the room, but she didn't go far. Something was dreadfully wrong and Mo wanted to be there, for Bev and for Gabriel, if there was anything she could do.

But the telephone conversation went on and on. Moving back into the hallway, Mo could see that Gabriel had already loosened his tie and mussed his hair, and the voice on the other end was so loud that she could tell that it wasn't Bev.

Alarmed, she looked up at Gabriel, silently asking to be let in on the situation.

It was clear that the other person was doing most of the talking. It was clear by the grim line of Gabriel's mouth that something was very, very wrong.

"Look, Harry," he said suddenly, forcefully. "I'm catching the next flight out. Don't do or say anything else. And don't upset Bev any more than you have already."

When he put the phone down, the room was suddenly silent. Much, much too silent.

"Mo," Gabriel said, his voice tired and edgy, "what exactly have you been doing with your spare time lately?"

She raised her head and swallowed hard. "That was Harry, wasn't it? What—what exactly did he say?"

For long moments Gabriel was silent. He looked down at the ground as if trying to get a grip on his emotions. Finally he took a deep breath.

"He said he didn't want to conduct his business in Chicago. He said he didn't want to live in Chicago. He said he never wanted to hear of Chicago again." Gabriel's words grew slightly louder with each sentence.

Mo opened her mouth to speak, but nothing came out. The feeling that her world had already exploded and she was just now beginning to feel the shattering pain was foremost in her mind.

"Is there more?" she eventually managed.

But of course there was. Bev wouldn't have been calling if Harry had simply been angry with Mo, if he had simply received the article, picked up the phone and dialed Chicago.

Gabriel motioned Mo to a chair, then dropped into one himself, stretching his legs out in front of him as he lowered his head to his chest and blew out a long puff of air.

"He's accused Bev of asking me to do whatever I could to convince him to move here. He's accused me of hiring you to do a sales pitch."

Mo took in a deep gulp of air and closed her eyes, but she could tell by the inflection in Gabriel's voice that he hadn't finished speaking.

When he hadn't yet continued, she opened her eyes and stared into Gabriel's face. His own eyes were darker than she'd ever seen them. And cold. Very cold.

"Harry's promised me that he will never, ever move his new family back to Chicago. If anything, he'll move them farther away. And if I follow him, he'll move again."

Mo covered her face with her hands, but Gabriel's voice went on, deep and hurting this time.

"He was calling her names, Mo, while I was on the phone. And he wouldn't put her on. He said that he hated kids, that he'd only ever tolerated her because of Nora."

"Gabriel," Mo said, reaching out her hand to touch the man she loved. But if he felt her touch, she couldn't tell. His chest was heaving, his fists were clenched. His eyes were blue flames. There was nothing she could do to help him.

For a moment Mo considered offering to talk to Harry herself, to try to explain, but she knew now that she wouldn't have anything he'd want to hear. She couldn't even begin to understand a man who would intentionally hurt a child that way. It was obvious that she'd only make the damage worse, if it could get any worse.

She wanted to say that she was sorry, but the word *sorry* was hopelessly inadequate at a time like this. "It's too late for sorry's," her father liked to say when he was upset with her, and for once she would have agreed with him.

"What will you do?" Mo forced herself to think of the here and now, of what little could be done.

Gabriel didn't answer right away. He stood there, his nostrils flaring, his hands curling into fists. When he finally spoke, his voice was tight, low, decisive... and he was more angry than she'd ever known him to be.

At once he jerked his head up and gazed into her face with glazed eyes.

"I'm going to her. Just as soon as I can get a flight out. I don't know what I'll do when I get there, but I'm damn well not going to let him talk to her—talk about her—like that again."

"You don't—you don't think he's hurt her? Physically?" Mo could barely get the words out, and she didn't want to say them to Gabriel, but they needed to be said.

"He swears that he hasn't touched her, and he knows I'd kill him if he did. But I've already called the police just to check things out. That won't make things any easier for her."

Gabriel looked at Mo as she covered her mouth with her hand.

"I'd better call the airline," he said at last, turning his back on her. "We'll talk when I get back."

Mo stood staring at him, stricken, wanting to ask if she could come with him, but knowing that he wouldn't want her around.

"Go to bed, Mo," he said when he hung up and found her still standing there. "Get some rest. There's nothing you can do now." She flinched at his words, and he swore softly.

"Go to bed. Please," he said again. "I'll be out of your way in thirty minutes." And without another look, he left the room, climbing the stairs to pack.

When he returned to find her still standing like a statue in the kitchen, Gabriel took a deep breath and dropped his head onto his chest. Mo could tell that he was hoping she would have hidden herself away before he left.

She saw him raise his hand as if to touch her hair. But he didn't. He didn't even come close. "Don't worry," he assured her. "If I have to call my attorney and take her away from Nora, I will. I'm not letting anyone hurt her that way. I'll tell you more when I know more. We'll talk," he repeated.

She nodded because it seemed the safest thing to do, and because any words she might have offered would only have stuck in her throat.

But as she watched him leave a short time later, Mo knew why she hadn't really committed herself to talking.

She wouldn't be here when he got back.

He was stunned and disoriented by the sudden turn of events right now. But when the reality and enormity of the consequences of Mo's actions had finally taken hold, Mo knew that Gabriel wouldn't want her here. That hope was gone. Completely.

Oh, he'd be nice. He'd be polite. Because he was Gabriel, and that was Gabriel's way. But he wouldn't touch her. He wouldn't want her around.

She had interfered; she had once again tried too hard to make things right. Only this time she had made things so wrong that both Gabriel and Bev were going to suffer. Harry was going to do his best to keep Gabriel from his daughter.

And Mo had arranged it all.

As she packed her bags, as she wrote her notes to both Gabriel and Aunt Rose, as she walked out the door, Mo knew that she had never made a greater mistake than she had when she had come to Gabriel's door.

Mo remembered all the times she'd tried to please her father only to have everything go wrong. Well, she had done it again. Only this time it was her fault, completely her fault. There was no one else to blame.

She had hurt—seriously hurt—the most important person in the world to her.

And now she had to begin the rest of her life—without him.

Chapter Ten

The house seemed oddly silent when Gabriel returned the next evening. He'd tried to call several times, but the machine had always kicked on. When he pushed open the door and called for Mo, to let her know that it was only him, no one answered.

"It's okay," he told himself. There was no reason to worry. She'd probably just tucked herself away in one of the rooms to work, or maybe she was asleep.

Gabe dropped his bags in the hallway, continuing up the stairs. An ominous sense of foreboding flooded through him as he moved through the house and still heard no evidence of human habitation.

"Mo, where are you?" he called.

At another time he might have felt foolish talking to what he was almost certain was an empty house. But what he'd half known last night, half figured out after arriving in St. Paul when he'd finally read her article, couldn't be ignored. Mo had been involved in the Harry episode, right up to her pretty auburn bangs. And she'd been severely distressed when he'd told her that Harry had been cruel to Bev. As upset as he had been, Gabriel remembered.

By now he knew her well enough to know she'd count herself completely responsible. She'd be feeling guilty, condemning her own actions. He knew as well as anyone how that felt. How a person could punish themselves for things that they really couldn't change.

"Mo!" he called again into the quiet.

A sudden spurt of fear and adrenaline sent him racing up the stairs, rushing down the hall to Mo's room.

There he found what he'd been afraid of. Emptiness. Nothing on the shelves except Rose's things. Mo's clothes were gone. Even more telling, her books and her computer were gone.

All that remained were two letters in her oversize swirling handwriting—one for him, one for Rose.

Swallowing, Gabriel picked up his own letter and opened it.

He knew what he'd find before he even read the words. She'd written a confession, an apology, and then had jotted down the number of an agency so that he could find a replacement for her.

Gabriel shook his head at that. Where did she think he could find a replacement for her, the woman who had ridden into his life in a rattletrap car, who'd made him laugh when he hadn't wanted to, touched off desires in him he'd thought he'd tossed out the window, who'd shared her special gifts and her affection with his lonely little child and who'd tried to bring his daughter back to him? He wouldn't find those things at an agency...or anywhere else on earth, except where Mo was.

And where *was* Mo? She didn't say where she was going. He didn't have the slightest idea where she was. She could be anywhere—across the street, scribbling away in the Yukon, on an island in the middle of the Pacific, on a cruise ship looking for the father for her child...

"Damn you, Mo. You could have waited," he said to the room, as if a part of her were still there and could hear what he needed to say. Why the hell hadn't she waited for him?

Without thinking twice, he took the letter for Rose. Rose was Mo's aunt, her family, someone she could confide in. With shaking fingers and no remorse, he ripped open the second letter. But when he read it, there was nothing new. The note was simple, an apology for not staying until Rose could return, a wish for the good health of mother and baby.

Gabriel paced the room. He slammed the door. He nearly put his fist through the wall. Where the hell was the woman? He didn't even know where her apartment was. He didn't have any way of contacting her.

He didn't know where she was, and probably no one else did either... except maybe Rose.

Rose.

Taking the stairs two at a time, Gabe dug out the number and began to dial, praying that Rose was at home and would be able to tell him something.

The phone rang ten times. A small child answered. In the confusion over who was calling, the phone was dropped. Twice.

Finally Gabriel heard the sound of Rose's familiar hello.

"She could be anywhere, Mr. Bonner," Rose said, when he was finally able to explain. "Mo hides to lick her wounds. It's her way. When she was little, she had a thousand places where she went to heal herself and to daydream. And as a woman, she's still got a number of places where she hides away to write now and then. Is it really important that you get in touch with her personally? Is there something you need her for? Something she didn't do? Maybe someone else... Or I could come back in just a little while—"

"Rose," Gabriel said, cutting her off. "I'm sorry. No one else. I need . . . Mo. Just Mo. You understand?"

I need to know she's safe, he wanted to say. *I need her in my arms, my bed. I need her to say she'll stay with me.*

"Well," Rose said, her voice hesitant, uncertain. "Yes, I think I do understand. Maybe. Do you care for her, then? A little?"

"A little? God, Rose, not a little, no. Too much."

There was silence on the line. Gabe could hear the ticking of the clock that matched the beat of his heart.

"I don't want her hurt," Rose said suddenly. "Don't go looking if you're not sure."

Gabriel counted to ten. He thanked God that there were other people who cared about Mo. But . . . "Tell me, Rose. Please. I'm afraid I may have already hurt her. I should have talked to her, taken her with me. I should have thought. Tell me what you know, where she might be, Rose," he urged. "I need her."

"You *love* her," Rose corrected, her voice growing more decisive. He could almost see her smile across the wires. "I always told her you were a smart man. But . . ."

Gabe heard her sigh.

"You're going to have to be *very* smart, Mr. Bonner," she told him. "Because, although there are a few places she might go, a half-dozen or so I can think of offhand, some of them—*most* of them—don't even have phones. It could take quite a while to find her if she's hidden herself away without a telephone."

And she would be alone, Gabriel thought, with nothing but her thoughts for company. She could be hurt with no one to call for help.

"Then we'd better get started," he said quietly.

"Yes. Yes, of course," the older woman said, responding to his determined tone. "Just one more thing, Mr. Bonner."

"What's that?"

"When Mo was a little girl, hiding up in a tree, she'd run away and hide again if anyone came near. If she's really hurting, if she *really* doesn't want to be found, well, you just might look a lifetime and never find her."

The cabin was cool this time of day, even though the sun filtered in through the needles of the two tall fir trees outside. A pine-scented breeze drifted in where Mo had cracked the window. Wisconsin this far north and well off the main roads was quiet. Except for the slight rustle of the wind through the trees and the soft twitter of the birds, the only sound was the sluggish drag of her pencil moving across the paper.

It should have been a perfect place to write, but all Mo saw when she looked down were the simple doodles that she had absentmindedly placed there.

And the memory of a face that she'd never see again.

The small snapping sound of her pencil lead breaking where she had pressed down on the paper too hard shot through the silence. Mo rubbed her forehead with the palm of her hand. It had happened again and again.

She couldn't write, not even in the cabin her uncle had slipped her the key to years ago. It was the most inspiring place she knew, a place where she could write and live the life she'd always wanted.

She *was* living the life she always wanted.

And almost all she had to show for it was a lot of broken pencils and a garbage can full of childish scribbles.

It had been two weeks since she had left Gabriel's house. For two weeks she had thought of him, dreamed of him, imagined him when she didn't want to.

The last time she had looked into his eyes he'd been wounded, hurting, reeling from the knowledge that she was the one who had ruined his small chance of bringing Bev back. By now he'd had time to think about it, to learn to hate her. He'd be alone in that huge house. He'd be beside himself with grief and impotent rage. She was the one who had done that to him, and then run away.

In another week or two, Aunt Rose would be back. Then she'd call, Mo promised herself, to ask about Gabriel. Because she needed to know that he was taking care of himself, that he was as well as could be expected.

And then, when she knew for sure that he would survive, she'd go on. She'd keep moving, she'd do... something.

Until then, there was work. Only work could help blot out the memories of Gabriel and his touch, his voice, his face that she could nearly reach out to.... Mo's eyes blurred as she bent to her paper again.

The sound of a vehicle on the weathered gravel road made her still her useless pencil. No one ever came out here.

Whoever it was, they were moving fast, the brakes groaning as they made the turn into her drive. It was probably someone who'd missed the last county road and was turning around, she thought.

But the crunch of tires on the rocky dirt farther up the drive, the slam of a car door, the sudden sound of a fist on wood, brought Mo to her feet, confused and disoriented.

"Are you in there, Mo? Open the door!" The banging began again.

Deep breaths, she ordered herself. Take deep breaths. It's not him. You're imagining things. It's a ranger here to tell me that someone dropped a match in the woods and started a small fire. Or it's Uncle John wanting his cabin back.

But when the pounding continued and Mo tiptoed to the window, she could see a familiar white Lincoln parked just off the dirt road.

Her heart began to thud. Faster and faster until it felt like it was climbing up out of her throat.

"Mo?" Gabriel called again. "Are you there?"

Wiping her hands down her jeans as though they were dirty, Mo took a breath. She moved slowly to the door, put the rusty chain in the latch and pulled the door open a crack.

Immediately her vision was filled with the sight of Gabriel, tall and lean, peering in at her through the narrow opening.

"Mo..." His voice felt like a caress. "Mo... I thought I might never find you. You must have been pure hell to beat at hide-and-seek when you were a kid."

His hand was on the door. If she curled her fingers around the edge, she could touch him—feel that he was real.

"You *could* let me in," he suggested, as though that were a possibility. Mo knew that it was not. She could only run away from him once, and if she opened the door now, she'd be begging him to forgive her when she hadn't even been able to forgive herself.

She shook her head. "Something's wrong, isn't it?" she asked. "Is that why you're here?"

"You know something's wrong," he told her. "As wrong as it gets."

"Bev?" she asked, swallowing. "Is it Bev? Or Rose?"

Gabriel shook his head. "Bev's fine," he assured her. "And Rose? She's in love with Colorado. The house didn't burn. You didn't leave all the lights on when you left. The ironing isn't piling up. Or if it is, I damn well don't care. That's not what's wrong, Mo."

She bit her lip to keep it from trembling. She clenched her fingers around the door. She did touch him then, just once with the tip of one finger.

He sucked in his breath and pushed on the door.

"Then—"

"The problem, Mo," Gabriel rasped in a harsh, choking voice, "is that you're on one side of the damn door and I'm on the other. Now, please, open up. Or tell me why you won't."

The lump in her throat was immense. "Because," she tried.

It was a little girl's answer. And Mo knew that for a man like Gabriel, it wouldn't be enough.

But what she was unprepared for was the way Gabriel's face suddenly blanched, the way he looked down the drive to where her car sat next to his.

"Mo," he whispered. "You're not— It isn't that you're not alone, is it?" The lines of his face were taut.

She blinked twice, his sudden change of subject catching her off guard.

"Is there someone else there with you?" he asked again.

Then Mo understood. Perfectly. She felt her face glow red. "You think I'm in here—reproducing?" she squeaked.

At her shocked tone, Gabriel visibly slumped. He rested his head on the door. "No, I think the reproducing usually comes after the touching. It was the touching I was worried about," he admitted sheepishly, his voice muffled by the wood.

"But, Mo," he began again, in those slow, coaxing tones that did such wicked things to her nerves. "If you're not— If you're alone, why won't you open the door? I want to be able to touch you while we talk."

It only took that to push her over the edge. Mo felt the teardrops slip from beneath her lids.

Gabriel swore out loud. A word she'd never heard him use before. He hit the door. Hard.

"Open the door, Mo. Right now."

Ashamed at her inability to control herself, Mo hid her face behind the door. "Go home, Gabriel," she said. "I hurt you, and I'm angry with myself. But if I open the door, then you'll be inside. And then I'll be crying on you and begging you to forgive me. I don't want to do that. I don't want to let you see me making a total fool of myself."

He closed his eyes. He put his head back, and she could see him swallow. "Cry on me, Mo. Please. And I'll hold you. I—I just want to hold you."

She raised her head and peeked through the opening.

Gabriel was pushing on the door so hard that the chain was as taut as it could get. He was staring at her with dark, purposeful eyes.

"But I promise you, Mo, if you don't open the door right now, if you don't take that damn chain off that's keeping us apart, I'm going to be the one making a fool of himself. Because I've never in my life tried to break a door down before. But I will. If you don't open up. Right now. So that I can be with you. So that I can wipe your tears away. So that I can kiss you. Right after I read you the riot act for running away in the first place."

Mo raised her head, and this time, when she looked into Gabriel's eyes, she saw something that she didn't trust herself to believe.

She looked at the door. It was solid, heavy, sturdy. Gabriel was a big man. Even so, he would never break it down. He probably knew that. But looking into his determined face, she knew that he'd try. And that he'd keep trying.

By rights he should hate her. She'd left the note. He knew what she'd done, but his words, the low, velvet tone of his voice, the soft seductive glint in his eyes, the steely determination of his fists as he reached back to swing at the door, were all she needed to tell her that hate wasn't what Gabriel was talking about right now.

With a small sniff, Mo nodded, closing the door to unlatch it.

When she pulled it back wide to let him in, he stepped over the threshold and threaded his fingers through her hair, pulling her to him in a kiss that was rough with untempered emotion. His lips sucked at hers, he banded her to him with his arms, he pressed her tightly to him, his thighs parting to pinion her own legs between them.

"Is this where the hell you've been the whole time, Mo?" he demanded, breaking away suddenly. "I've been everywhere, looking for you. If I hadn't found you soon, I think I might have gone totally out of my mind with worry. Didn't you think about that? Didn't you? You must have known. And even if you didn't know I loved you, you must have known I at least cared."

A shudder went through Gabriel as he kissed her again, not waiting for her to answer. He raked suddenly gentle thumbs across her cheeks where her tears had tracked down. Then he gathered her to him, so close that she could barely move.

But that didn't matter. She didn't want to move.

"Gabriel," Mo whispered against his lips when he released her. "You can't still want me after I wrecked everything. I—I wanted so badly to make things right for you and Bev, but I tried way too hard. I ruined your little girl's life. How could you possibly love me? How could you care at all?"

She pressed her head to his chest, breathing in the air that surrounded him.

Gabriel snuggled her closer, swaying with her in his arms.

"You didn't wreck anything," he told her in a voice that was softer than the air. "And you could never hurt me or Bev by trying to make things right for us."

When she tried to shake her head, he stopped her with a kiss that effectively imprisoned her and held her still. Pulling back to look at her, he smoothed one hand beneath her hair, massaging her neck.

"Nora dumped Harry," he told her in a still, husky voice. "And she's even agreed to move back to Chicago for Bev's sake. I think the article you sent really shook her up. She felt guilty that you were trying to do something for her daughter while she was the one who'd been fooled by Harry's attentions. Looks like you worked another miracle," he whispered with a small smile, dropping a kiss on her jawline.

"You won't have custody, will you?" Mo asked sympathetically, remembering his comment the night he had flown off to St. Paul.

"No." Gabriel shook his head. "I don't want to stir things up for Bev right now. Her mother is beginning to loosen up a bit, but I think Nora will always be a bit jealous. I don't want her to get scared and fly again. This is the best we can hope for. Bev and I will be together a lot now, especially since Nora wants to continue with her work."

Mo smiled back at him then and touched her lips to his chin. "Then I'm glad for you."

He turned his head so that his lips met hers, then pushed back to gaze into her face. "I'd still love you, even if things hadn't worked out, you know. Nothing would stop me from caring."

Mo's eyes brimmed over, with happiness this time. "You know that I love you, too?" she asked softly.

"I wanted to hear it," he said, his eyes growing fierce and possessive. "But I knew that there was something between us. You didn't have to send that article to Harry. It wasn't in your job description. You did it for me and Bev, didn't you?" At her small nod, Gabriel's brows rose. "And," he added, "you went to a party that I know darn well you didn't want to attend. And you did it just for me."

Mo looked at him solemnly, sliding up and placing her hands on his chest. On her toes, she wasn't quite on eye level with him, but it was close enough. "I *did* want to go to the ball," she said slowly.

Gabriel ducked his head in disbelief. "You were terrified. You were nervous."

"I was petrified, shaking in my shoes," she agreed. "But I wanted to go. I wanted to be your Cinderella. I wanted to be beautiful for you."

As Mo finished her last sentence, Gabriel groaned, scooping her into his arms and depositing her on a high table. He spread her thighs and fit himself between them, bringing her as close as he could.

"You were always beautiful to me," he said fiercely, bending his head to nip her neck. "I was just too big a fool, too cautious, too afraid I'd make the same mistakes I'd made before. I was always living on the edge, scared to death I'd let things go too far with you, hurt you somehow. When you left..." Gabe looked to the heavens, blinking his eyes, his hands tightening slightly on her shoulders. "When you left," he said more softly, "I knew I'd waited too long to admit what I think I'd always known. Life is just too empty without you, Mo. Will you marry me?"

Mo looked deep into the eyes of this man who was life to her, this man who filled her with joy and hope. She couldn't imagine a world without him, her life going on day after day without him there. But it was so hard to believe that he loved her back... even though he'd said the words.

"Mo," Gabriel whispered. "I'll give you children, if I can. I can promise you that. I will. With you... Well, I know you'd never hurt a child. We'd give them love, you and I... if you'll marry me, that is."

His words were filled with conviction. He meant every syllable, Mo knew. She remembered that day when he'd had to tell Bev that their time was up. She remembered thinking that he would never have another, that no woman who loved him could ever ask him to have another child. Mo knew with every ounce of her being that this man, her Gabriel, was offering her the greatest gift she'd ever have—his total, unconditional love.

Tears filled her eyes, and she took his face into her hands. She kissed his eyelids, and then his mouth. "I would never require you to do that for me, Gabriel," she promised. "Loving you, being with you—it's all I'll ever need."

Gabriel sucked in a deep breath of air and dropped a kiss on the top of her head. "Come on, Cinderella, let's go get married. I don't want to wait any longer," he said, grinning down at her as he slid her off the table and spun her around in his arms.

Mo looked around the idyllic cabin that had been too much like a prison, then back at Gabriel. "Let's go home," she agreed. "I'll pack my things."

Smiling, Gabriel nodded, then moved aside to let her do whatever she had to do to get ready.

But as she moved, Mo saw that he had stopped, still, his attention riveted to the wall on the far side of the room. She felt her cheeks begin to grow warm.

"You've been busy. Writing again," he said, looking at the mostly empty bits of paper hanging from strips of tape.

"No." She shook her head, motioning to the four paper bags filled with crumpled-up sheets from legal pads. "Mostly I've been destroying trees. And thinking of you."

But Gabriel's attention had been caught by something on that wall, and even Mo's tugging on his sleeve couldn't hold him back. He moved across the room, stopping suddenly. Mo didn't need to look to see what Gabriel had found.

The single large scrap of paper with its awkward picture-book drawings and heartfelt words was the only thing she'd been able to write in the time she'd been gone.

Gabriel moved closer and placed his hand on the wall beside it.

"'Somewhere there is a house, a wonderful house, Gabriel's house,'" he read out loud. "'And in the house, there is a kitchen, a kitchen filled with sunshine and cinnamon and spun sugar. And in the kitchen, a child with sparkling eyes and ballerina feet. And a man, Gabriel, strong and tall, who feeds the child strawberries and stories and hugs. He smiles at the child. And the child smiles back. For she knows that in Gabriel's house . . . in her father's house . . . there is love. Always love.' ''

As the words died on his lips, Gabriel turned to Mo. He was across the room, ten feet away, but as he looked at her, studied her, his heart touched hers as surely as his hands had ever touched her skin. Tenderly. Reverently.

"There always will be, Mo," he said. "I promise you there always will be love in our house."

Epilogue

It had been a long labor, longer than Mo had expected, considering how much practice she'd had the last few years.

As Gabriel turned from the phone the nurse had brought into the room, Mo smiled at him. "Is everything all right?"

"As right as it gets," he agreed with a grin. "Bev says that Sarah is taking a nap and Matt has found something 'interesting' to do with glue and paper. If you want to know the details—"

"I don't think so," she said, laughing and stopping him with a touch of her hand. "I trust Bev. If it's a mess, she'll clean it up before we get home. She didn't mind missing her date too much?"

"What date?" Gabriel asked, running a hand through his hair. He glanced over to where the nurse was cleaning up his new baby daughter. "Bev's too young to go out with boys," he growled, watching the newborn's tiny arms and legs wave in the air as the baby mewed her displeasure.

"I didn't mean that kind of date," Mo soothed, running her hand over the tense muscles of his arm. "Nora told me that Bev and a group of her girlfriends were going down to the Art Institute."

Gabriel nodded curtly at that, smiling sheepishly. "That's not a date," he accused.

"It certainly is," Mo said, tossing her head as best she could from the hospital bed. "Just because there isn't a male involved doesn't mean it's not important," she teased.

"Okay, you're right," he agreed. "But I guess Bev didn't mind the change of plans. She sounded totally, absolutely thrilled about the baby."

Mo laughed at that. Bev had practically done handsprings down the street when they told her they were having a third child.

"I hope that you're happy, too," she said, suddenly serious. "I promise this one will be the last. I can't keep making babies forever."

Gabriel settled himself in the chair next to her bed as the nurse brought the squirming little bundle of lungs and limbs and a tiny spot of hair and placed it in Mo's arms. He leaned nearer to Mo as she snuggled Amanda close.

"I'm not complaining about our baby." He whispered low so that no harm would come to such tiny little eardrums. "I love every one of them, completely. You know I couldn't love them more, even if I do hate having to see you go through what you do to bring one into the world. Besides," he said, placing his lips near Mo's ear, as if the baby could really understand. "I'm taking full credit for this little bundle myself. I don't remember exactly *planning* this one, do you?"

Mo shook her head and turned so that Gabriel could kiss her. "No," she agreed when they finally parted. "I don't remember planning another child."

"In fact," Gabriel said with a slow smile, "if I recall at all correctly, this baby was conceived one night when I totally lost my head in the arms of a woman. A naked woman with fire in her eyes and long, beautiful legs," he added. "Do you happen to recall that, by any chance?"

A sexy shrug that sent her hospital gown off her shoulder was Mo's answer. Then she twisted her lips as though she were trying to dredge up the past. "I'm not quite sure. I think I might remember losing my head a little bit myself one night. But if that's true, then I'm sorry. I know how you like to be in control, totally in control," she said, repeating the words he'd once said to her in another place and time.

Reaching out, Gabriel touched the small fist of his child, a fist that was no bigger than his thumb. Turning, he kissed his wife, hard and swift.

"That was long ago," he admitted. "Long ago. Since I met you, since you came into my world, the most wonderful memories I have are of times when I wasn't thinking clearly at all. And I don't worry much about making mistakes anymore."

He smoothed his thumb over the silky skin of his daughter's arm.

"Whatever we do, Mo, everything we do together," he said, in a voice grown tight with emotion, "will always be right."

"Even making babies?" Mo asked, raising her eyebrows to tease him.

Gabriel growled low in his throat and kissed her again. "*Especially* making babies," he agreed.

* * * * *

COMING NEXT MONTH

#1048 ANYTHING FOR DANNY—Carla Cassidy
Under the Mistletoe—Fabulous Fathers
Danny Morgan had one wish this Christmas—to reunite his divorced parents. But Sherri and Luke Morgan needed more than their son's hopes to bring them together. They needed to rediscover their long-lost love.

#1049 TO WED AT CHRISTMAS—Helen R. Myers
Under the Mistletoe
Nothing could stop David Shepherd and Harmony Martin from falling in love—though their feuding families struggled to keep them apart. Would it take a miracle to get them married?

#1050 MISS SCROOGE—Toni Collins
Under the Mistletoe
"Bah, humbug" was all lonely Casey Tucker had to say about the holidays. But that was before handsome Gabe Wheeler gave her the most wonderful Christmas gift of all....

#1051 BELIEVING IN MIRACLES—Linda Varner
Under the Mistletoe—Mr. Right, Inc.
Andy Fulbright missed family life, and Honey Truman needed a father for her son. Their convenient marriage fulfilled their common needs, but would love fulfill their dreams?

#1052 A COWBOY FOR CHRISTMAS—Stella Bagwell
Under the Mistletoe
Spending the holidays with cowboy Chance Delacroix was a joy Lucinda Lambert knew couldn't last. She was a woman on the run, and leaving was the only way to keep Chance out of danger.

#1053 SURPRISE PACKAGE—Lynn Bulock
Under the Mistletoe
Miranda Dalton needed a miracle to save A Caring Place shelter. What she got was Jared Tarkett. What could a sexy drifter teach *her* about life, love and commitment?

MILLION DOLLAR SWEEPSTAKES (III)

No purchase necessary. To enter, follow the directions published. Method of entry may vary. For eligibility, entries must be received no later than March 31, 1996. No liability is assumed for printing errors, lost, late or misdirected entries. Odds of winning are determined by the number of eligible entries distributed and received. Prizewinners will be determined no later than June 30, 1996.

Sweepstakes open to residents of the U.S. (except Puerto Rico), Canada, Europe and Taiwan who are 18 years of age or older. All applicable laws and regulations apply. Sweepstakes offer void wherever prohibited by law. Values of all prizes are in U.S. currency. This sweepstakes is presented by Torstar Corp., its subsidiaries and affiliates, in conjunction with book, merchandise and/or product offerings. For a copy of the Official Rules send a self-addressed, stamped envelope (WA residents need not affix return postage) to: MILLION DOLLAR SWEEPSTAKES (III) Rules, P.O. Box 4573, Blair, NE 68009, USA.

EXTRA BONUS PRIZE DRAWING

No purchase necessary. The Extra Bonus Prize will be awarded in a random drawing to be conducted no later than 5/30/96 from among all entries received. To qualify, entries must be received by 3/31/96 and comply with published directions. Drawing open to residents of the U.S. (except Puerto Rico), Canada, Europe and Taiwan who are 18 years of age or older. All applicable laws and regulations apply; offer void wherever prohibited by law. Odds of winning are dependent upon number of eligible entries received. Prize is valued in U.S. currency. The offer is presented by Torstar Corp., its subsidiaries and affiliates in conjunction with book, merchandise and/or product offering. For a copy of the Official Rules governing this sweepstakes, send a self-addressed, stamped envelope (WA residents need not affix return postage) to: Extra Bonus Prize Drawing Rules, P.O. Box 4590, Blair, NE 68009, USA.

SWP-S1194

JINGLE BELLS, WEDDING BELLS:
Silhouette's Christmas Collection for 1994

Christmas Wish List

*To beat the crowds at the malls and get the perfect present for *everyone,* even that snoopy Mrs. Smith next door!

*To get through the holiday parties without running my panty hose.

*To bake cookies, decorate the house and serve the perfect Christmas dinner—just like the women in all those magazines.

*To sit down, curl up and read my Silhouette Christmas stories!

Join *New York Times* bestselling author Nora Roberts, along with popular writers Barbara Boswell, Myrna Temte and Elizabeth August, as we celebrate the joys of Christmas—and the magic of marriage—with

JINGLE BELLS, WEDDING BELLS

Silhouette's Christmas Collection for 1994.

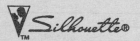

HARLEQUIN® 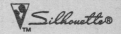Silhouette®

The movie event of the season can be the reading event of the year!

Lights... The lights go on in October when CBS presents Harlequin/Silhouette Sunday Matinee Movies. These four movies are based on bestselling Harlequin and Silhouette novels.

Camera... As the cameras roll, be the first to read the original novels the movies are based on!

Action... Through this offer, you can have these books sent directly to you! Just fill in the order form below and you could be reading the books...before the movie!

48288-4	Treacherous Beauties by Cheryl Emerson		
		$3.99 U.S./$4.50 CAN.	☐
83305-9	Fantasy Man by Sharon Green		
		$3.99 U.S./$4.50 CAN.	☐
48289-2	A Change of Place by Tracy Sinclair		
		$3.99 U.S./$4.50CAN.	☐
83306-7	Another Woman by Margot Dalton		
		$3.99 U.S./$4.50 CAN.	☐

TOTAL AMOUNT	$	
POSTAGE & HANDLING	$	
($1.00 for one book, 50¢ for each additional)		
APPLICABLE TAXES*	$	_____
TOTAL PAYABLE	$	_____
(check or money order—please do not send cash)		

To order, complete this form and send it, along with a check or money order for the total above, payable to Harlequin Books, to: **In the U.S.:** 3010 Walden Avenue, P.O. Box 9047, Buffalo, NY 14269-9047; **In Canada:** P.O. Box 613, Fort Erie, Ontario, L2A 5X3.

Name: _____

Address: _____ City: _____

State/Prov.: _____ Zip/Postal Code: _____

*New York residents remit applicable sales taxes.
Canadian residents remit applicable GST and provincial taxes.

CBSPR

"HOORAY FOR HOLLYWOOD" SWEEPSTAKES

HERE'S HOW THE SWEEPSTAKES WORKS

OFFICIAL RULES — NO PURCHASE NECESSARY

To enter, complete an Official Entry Form or hand print on a 3" x 5" card the words "HOORAY FOR HOLLYWOOD", your name and address and mail your entry in the pre-[...] or to: "Hooray for Hollywood" Sweepstakes, P.O. Box [...] 269-9076 or "Hooray for Hollywood" Sweepstakes, P.O. Box 637, [...] Erie, Ontario L2A 5X3. Entries must be sent via First Class Mail and be received no later than 12/31/94. No liability is assumed for lost, late or misdirected mail.

Winners will be selected in random drawings to be conducted no later than January 31, 1995 from all eligible entries received.

Grand Prize: A 7-day/6-night trip for 2 to Los Angeles, CA including round trip air transportation from commercial airport nearest winner's residence, accommodations at the Regent Beverly Wilshire Hotel, free rental car, and $1,000 spending money. (Approximate prize value which will vary dependent upon winner's residence: $5,400.00 U.S.); 500 Second Prizes: A pair of "Hollywood Star" sunglasses (prize value: $9.95 U.S. each). Winner selection is under the supervision of D.L. Blair, Inc., an independent judging organization, whose decisions are final. Grand Prize travelers must sign and return a release of liability prior to traveling. Trip must be taken by 2/1/96 and is subject to airline schedules and accommodations availability.

Sweepstakes offer is open to residents of the U.S. (except Puerto Rico) and Canada who are 18 years of age or older, except employees and immediate family members of Harlequin Enterprises, Ltd., its affiliates, subsidiaries, and all agencies, entities or persons connected with the use, marketing or conduct of this sweepstakes. All federal, state, provincial, municipal and local laws apply. Offer void wherever prohibited by law. Taxes and/or duties are the sole responsibility of the winners. Any litigation within the province of Quebec respecting the conduct and awarding of prizes may be submitted to the Regie des loteries et courses du Quebec. All prizes will be awarded; winners will be notified by mail. No substitution of prizes are permitted. Odds of winning are dependent upon the number of eligible entries received.

Potential grand prize winner must sign and return an Affidavit of Eligibility within 30 days of notification. In the event of non-compliance within this time period, prize may be awarded to an alternate winner. Prize notification returned as undeliverable may result in the awarding of prize to an alternate winner. By acceptance of their prize, winners consent to use of their names, photographs, or likenesses for purpose of advertising, trade and promotion on behalf of Harlequin Enterprises, Ltd., without further compensation unless prohibited by law. A Canadian winner must correctly answer an arithmetical skill-testing question in order to be awarded the prize.

For a list of winners (available after 2/28/95), send a separate stamped, self-addressed envelope to: Hooray for Hollywood Sweepstakes 3252 Winners, P.O. Box 4200, Blair, NE 68009.

CBSRLS

"Hooray for Hollywood"
SWEEPSTAKES!

Yes, I'd love to win the Grand Prize — a vacation in Hollywood — or one of 500 pairs of "sunglasses of the stars"! Please enter me in the sweepstakes!

This entry must be received by December 31, 1994

Winners will be notified b

Name _____

Address _____ Apt. _____

City _____

State/Prov. _____ Zip/Postal Code _____

Daytime phone number _____
                                    (area code)

Mail all entries to: Hooray for Hollywood Sweepstakes,
P.O. Box 9076, Buffalo, NY 14269-9076.
In Canada, mail to: Hooray for Hollywood Sweepstakes,
P.O. Box 637, Fort Erie, ON L2A 5X3.

KCH

OFFICIAL ENTRY COUPON

"Hooray for Hollywood"
SWEEPSTAKES!

Yes, I'd love to win the Grand Prize — a vacation in Hollywood — or one of 500 pairs of "sunglasses of the stars"! Please enter me in the sweepstakes!

This entry must be received by December 31, 1994.

Winners will be notified by January 31, 1995.

Name _____

Address _____ Apt. _____

City _____

State/Prov. _____ Zip/Postal Code _____

Daytime phone number _____
                                    (area code)

Mail all entries to: Hooray for Hollywood Sweepstakes,
P.O. Box 9076, Buffalo, NY 14269-9076.
In Canada, mail to: Hooray for Hollywood Sweepstakes,
P.O. Box 637, Fort Erie, ON L2A 5X3.

KCH